The Contract

The Contract

BIJU VASUDEVAN

PARTRIDGE
A Penguin Random House Company

To order additional copies of this book, contact
Partridge India
000 800 10062 62
orders.india@partridgepublishing.com

www.partridgepublishing.com/india

To Little "Buttons" & "Kochu"

'Sometimes God calms the storm, but sometimes God lets the storm rage and calms His child. –

Leslie Gould

"First of all I would like to thank the Almighty for inspiring me and for protecting the handwritten manuscript from ravages of time and termites for a long period of more than fifteen years. I thank my Wife for putting up with my eccentricities and believing in me and also for the second proof reading. I am grateful to the lady typist who decoded my contorted cryptic handwriting and managed to somehow convert my handwritten manuscript into typeset.

I thank the "Dai Gohonzon" for forgiving my sins and giving me the "Mystic Opportunity through practice of The Mystic Law" without which fruition of this effort would not have taken place.

I express my heartfelt gratitude to all my Teachers and my English Teachers Mrs. Meera Pradhan and Mr. E A D-Costa in particular, who during my formative years, made a Non-Native Speaker of English like me, to achieve a fair degree of dexterity with the language that the world understands.

I thank the "Soka Gakkai International", "Bharat Soka Gakkai" and Sensei Ikeda for initiating me into Spiritual Practice to become a "Soka Victor".

I am grateful to my family, friends and colleagues for their support and encouragement.

Preface

Absolutely no research has gone into the Writing of this Book.

It is just the flight of feverish rampant imagination of a Young Man, who wanted to be an Author, but was forced by circumstances to do something else.

There was no access to internet in those days and whatever information you could glean had to be sourced from magazines and newspapers. If anything can be called a work of fiction, this is it. Pure unadulterated, unalloyed, figment of imagination.

So evidently, any resemblance to any person, character or place or event is purely coincidental and unintentional. And such instances indeed, shall be few and far in between.

I was about 25 when I wrote this. I had completed my Graduation in Mechanical Engineering and had landed a stable job in a State Run Enterprise, Steel Authority of India Ltd. But my Heart lay somewhere else. I wanted to become a Poet. And indeed I did churn out an explosion of colorful and imaginative poetry and had dutifully sent them to publishers only to be met with nonchalance. Some did not even bother to write back.

Then somebody told me that there is no market for poetry anymore. So I began writing this book. I believe it took me about six months to complete this.

But Mama was not Happy about all this. "If you continue to write, one day you will starve. Your Sister is growing older and we need to get her married off. Money is now required much more than ever before. So, it will suit you if you divorce yourself from your delusions and utopias and come to the real world and concentrate on your job and get raises."

I heeded her advice and put this in Cold Storage. Anyway, after completing the book, I did not know what to do with it next.

18 Years down the line, during a House Change, this handwritten manuscript suddenly resurfaced intact. Surprisingly the ravages of time and transport were not very evident. I was overjoyed at the serendipity but still did not know what to do with it.

Then one day, I saw this piece about Partridge that gave me ideas....................

In this I have faithfully reproduced what I had written as a Young Man without any major deviations. I sincerely hope that the dreamers and romantics of the world are with me in my endeavor.

Chapter 1

The damp stillness of the morning air was sliced open by the tumultuous clutter of a spheroid deformed beer can as it clattered along serpentine walkways. It scattered and startled the morning calm out of the wayward fowls and partridges.

It is shanty down Medellin. The crime capital of world. The paradise as well as last refuge for of the world's smugglers, drug gunners, flesh peddlers, cocaine dealers and of people assimilated in every nefarious, criminal and antisocial streams of the twentieth century.

Sun God has blessed his children once again with the curtsy call in the east and heavens had dyed themselves crimson to give their lord a red carpet welcome. The birds enthused up a welcome melody and the chimneys sent up curlers in abeyance.

Young Juan could not enjoy these opulence's of nature, these heavenly extravaganzas'. He had never been trained to do so. After all you were not supposed to enjoy life once you chose the shanty town man as your father. His initiations to the riddle of Human Existence included a concentrated concoction of obedience, concentration, discipline and an almost cowardly fear for the Almighty General Manager of Destiny also called Mr. God. Right now all his attentive faculties had telescoped unto the jagged deformed tin, merrily dancing away at his teasing feet. It was the cynosure of all his senses, the focal point of his existence at that moment.

The can rolled on with stoical nonchalance and occasionally pierced the monotony of dirt and filth around it with brilliant flashes of kaleidoscopic rainbow flashes when the infant rays of the young sun struck on its skinned edges. Slowly but resolutely it weaved its way among the piles of stones that had been set out as markers, under the able surveillance and guidance of Juan's leathered boot. Time and again it tried to stray from its premeditated path but the deft touch of Juan's foot forced it back in line.

As his makeshift ball made merry, Juan reflected upon the objectives of the every morning toils of his. He had some photographs of his football idol Emilio. Both the resplendent laminated ones on the show-windows of prominent sports stores and also the less glamorous, but more purposeful black and white ones in cheap, second rate sports magazines. Somehow he could only identify with the black and white version. He had scoured and digested all literature he could glean about Emilio. He had read enough to know that Emilio too had a similar background as him. His roots too lay in shanty-town, La-paz and from there it has been an inexorable climb against providence to the summit.

Young Juan was determined to trace out Emilio's footsteps. Emilio's feet had never touched anything soft when he was ten. It was with a battered old tin that he laid foundations upon which he created an edifice of mastery, dexterity and strength, ranging from superhuman to almost in-human, which enabled him to be the colossus that he was now.

Juan therefore abhorred the 'Cosco Marie' synthetic amateur football that his brothers Pedro had given him on his tenth birthday. In a moment supreme of resoluteness and determination he had slashed it open with his Swiss Army pen-knife, also a gift from Pedro. He had to divorce the temptation of a soft, round, even, predictable ball. He had to be prepared for the unexpected. His tender feet first needed the toughness that can only be provided by the jagged edges of a smashed beer can. If Emilio could do it why could not he.

The smashed can winded its way inexorably to the finish point of Juan's morning dribble course interspersed with pebble pyramids to be dodged across. Juan was in fact confused about what he should do. He seemed to be fit for just about everything. He had the tall noses the square chin the median chin cleft and piercing blue eyes of Mega Film Star Carlos whose life-size cut outs adorned every bus stop in down-town Medellin. He stood for all that a boy could aspire for, all that a man could ever be, an epitome of manhood and a national hero.

Juan had the longest kick in the shanty town. He could also rattle off the church rhymes and complex psalms faster and more accurately than everybody else. Poor Juan, there were so many things to do and only him, one poor boy, to do them all.

He was also a good shot with the sawed off shot-gun. He could accurately hit a pot at a distance of 30 yards. But that was potatoes compared to Pedro's aim.

"Oh! Pedro!!!", the most wonderful, beautiful, brother anybody can ever have. Big, strong, handsome and assertively masculine on his 500 CC turbocharged mean-machine; Pedro too could easily pass off as a teen idol.

But what puzzled and flabbergasted him were the routine absences of Pedro from the household.

The atmosphere of the house would stiffen a week before Pedro's departure as a harbinger perhaps. Talking would be rationed and laughing prohibited. There would be a stagnancy in the air like the lull before the storm. Then the day would arrive when a weeping mother and sister would say goodbye to Pedro as he clambered up into the back of an ash colored Pickup with his motorcycle hauled in after him. Then a sea change would come into the affairs of the house. Mother would ensconce herself in the canopy overseeing the family altar and seek Almighty's patronage. No food no drink, maybe for days. A copious supply of fears and prayers mumbled out half inaudibly from her trembling weather beaten scaly lips.

Sister Juanita would also weave around her a zone of apprehensive, yet eloquent silence. She would at once transform from the blossoming bloom that she was, to a withered trampled bouquet. Sleep for her would be a scarcity and the winks she gathered were interspersed with shrieks and nightmares. More often than not she would awaken the entire neighborhood with shrill ululations of foreboding and trepidation as she battled on in a nerve-wracking contest between her and the demon of her dreams. She would swear, bite, tear and rail upon her Ogre of imagination. Sometimes she would somnambulate and move around in a stupor muttering "Lord Christ" under her breath,… sometimes she would fall on her feet and offer herself to sacrifice at some imaginary altar. The whole home would become an accumulation of confusion and terror during Pedro's absence that ranged from one to two days to almost a full week.

The tumbling mass of contorted tin suddenly revolted against the despotic rule of Juan's feet and flashed past a stone mini pyramid via the wrong path.

'Damn it' Juan cursed under his breath "My rotten feet, if they gonna play any more tricky I ought to hack them off. No room for any bloody fucking mistakes man! Absolutely no room for any bloody fucking mistake. *Either mistake or you. First mistake is last mistake in poor man's life*"

So had father said. Must be true as Father is always correct. Fathers said "Poor Man must fight the Rich for his life and living. In a fight there is no compromise for mistakes. There is no place for them."

He had said "Fight is not just the fight you see on the street. Not just knives, bullets, blow pipes and poison darts. Fight my Boy! Is in everything you do. *A Rich Man lives while a Poor Man fights.* Everything he does is a battle for being and everything he does is to be taken as a fight."

He had said "So learn to fight. Lil Boy, Never too early to learn things. Learn to fight with body as well as mind. Never give up. At least God gives you a chance to fight. Some others get not even that."

Father also often used to say "*This is a one in a million world.* Only one man in a million is lucky enough to reach where he wants the straight way. Others have to 'hook and crook' to where they want to be and most of us aren't fortunate enough to be among those one in a million who are able to serve Christ in his true spirit."

The end of his arduous journey had finally come. At a furlongs distance he could see the white flutter of a torn underwear he had strung on a stake to act as the end marker. Now the stretch was straight like a bullet. He would go to the end to kick the tin over into the sewer and that would be the end of the practice session. Next morning it would be a re-run of the events, a photocopy to be reproduced in exact detail except for one finer point. A new beer can would take the place of the battered one trundling along at his feet. And beer cans, he found plenty. At the backyard of the bar, the delinquents mall, the teenage park, outside cinemas and just about anywhere. The beer cans were as ubiquitous in downtown Medellin as the omnipresent Mafioso.

'So no worry as to supply of raw materials' he through." Thank God for beer and so many people who like to drink if off cans!" Without them his recreation of Emilio would be incomplete.

End line was approaching soon a burst of energy a leaping crescendo of metabolic activity culminating in a soul felt kick sending the tin plummeting and sailing gracefully into the sewer and the torture quota for today would be over. The moment came and Juan did the needful and waited for the splash that the tin would make, as it made contact with the viscous rivalry of the sewage water. But there was none. Instead there was a dull thud followed by a ear-spattering clang as the tin mass at first struck some padded surface and then the gravel.

Juan looked up and froze in his footsteps, paralyzed by an overwhelming force of distress and misgiving at the unforeseen and capricious turn of events.

Chapter 2

Eyes met eyes and the accompanying glances locked and adhered to one another.

Before poor Juan loomed the irrepressible Lopez, the toughest and most feared man in entire Medellin shanty town. Harrowing tales of his cold-bloodedness and heartlessness had assumed folk lore status among shanty town folk. And there he stood before Juan, a bit perplexed, a bit amused and definitely very very angry. Juan had insulted him by kicking at him. And insult demanded satisfaction. Juan knew that there is going to be no mercy. So he simply stared at Fate.

Majestic Lopez stood before him, hands on hips, in full regalia. His oversized thigh and calf muscles strained and grappled with the uncompromising leather of his glistening black pant. A 'Dynamo power Blitz' macho-belt kept his devil insigne T-shirt to his waist. The devil mosaic on his chest seemed to mock in glee at Juan through its toothless jaws. Black Army riding boots complete with stirrups completed the outfit of His Majesty.

Lopez looked down upon Juan and his slit mouth opened slightly at a corner to expose tobacco stained jagged teeth. His cruel face contorted into a devilish grin and his mesmeric steely eyes wove a spider's web around Juan from which there was no escape. Juan felt like a rat cornered by a rattle snake, unable to fight back, unable to make a run. All he could do was just wait.

Suddenly the scars on Lopez's face grew prominent and he spat squarely on Juan's face.

"Day dreaming, young bastard, where is the sucker bitch who ditch delivered you??"

Juan opened his mouth to counsel for defense but not a word came out. His tongue seemed to be glued to his palate and try as hard he might, he could not free it.

"Son of a gun, son of a bitch, dreaming during day and you forget who rules here"

No Reply

"Blast it, Got no mouth bastard?. Wanna me knock out teeth to unlock your mouth. Or wanna me shut it for good".

Still no reply.

"Ya fuck yar sister, ya got no others thing to play with except this goddamned piece of bullet metal?"

Suddenly Juan found his voice.

"I played because Emilio plays. Errrrrr…. Sorry because tin plays Emilio."

"Ya in line with that bastard Emilio? That fucker who doomed our fatherland".

"I love him still, he played with tins you know, when he was small as me. So I play with tins, Sorry Sir. But tins help you kick harder. So Sorry Sir".

"Ya'll be sorry when I'll show ya how to kick hard, so don't worry."

"Sorry sir, sorry sir", the words reverberated in his larynx as though some biological gramophone disc had got stuck in his speech center of the cerebrum.

A cloud came over Lopez's countenance and his rattlesnake eyes narrowed. His forehead furrowed into countless ridges and shallow valleys and cheeks bulged out as adrenalin poured into his veins. The bulges of his pants grow rock hard as his right foot took off the ground kicking dust and dirt into the sewer behind as it launched itself into a back ward curl in space to gain momentum.

Juan stared on now into the space through which Lopez's leg cavorted and gyrated in its lethal dance, a sacrificial goat watching the Henchman's blade come down, slowly but surely on its neck.

The blow came for sure and the force of incursion was much more than expected. The bull hide tip of Lopez's boot jackknifed into his entrails and Juan buckled under it. He felt as though a grenade had burst in his stomach. Then came the resounding impact of Lopez's clenched steel fist square on the jaw. Juan's brain revolted with torture as his jaw seemed to decapitate. A salty taste overwhelmed his throat as though he had swallowed half of the Mediterranean. Blinking flares seemed to explode into his face as the entire creation seemed to spin and spiral around him in a damning dance of destruction, a frenzy of vengeance. Another blow and hot steamy blood spewed out from Juan's nose copiously. He felt his legs buckle under him. The exploding lights were being devoured by a monstrous curtain of red and black. Juan was sinking. Lopez swung again but missed. Juan had had enough. Soon the blinking white bodies were engulfed by a red and black monster. Curtain was falling, light was blacking out.

'One in a million, One in a million' a feverish faint voice seemed to sing in Juan's ears. Then lights went out. The dust settled around him.

Chapter 3

The sun beat down upon its earthly subjects and with consummate afternoon vigor. It invaded every house and shanty it could find and its rays encroached and captured every orifice or transparency in sight with a radiant vengeance. Juan's medium size shanty was not to be spared.

In streamed the hot scorching rays through the wide cleft in the makeshift window of Juan's room and caressed his face in a steamy embrace.

Consciousness dawned upon Juan with a dull sensation of retching and revolting of the entire body and an explicable warmth on the face. More sensibility infused into his body as his overworked nerve fibers strained to inject copious amounts of hormones into his blood stream. Presently the heat and the sanguine glow in the eyes become unbearable and he became aware of the irritation in his lachrymal glands due to the heat. He wanted to turn over. Mind sent body the instruction and the body made a vague attempt. But the real response to the command came as a spasm of unbearable shuddering pain that raked up the entire body. Mind responded with a smothered whimper.

Juan was fighting to hold back tears. ***Real men never cry. Not even when alone.*** But he could not. The hot fluid testimony of torment burst forth from his eyes, traced rivulets on his swollen cheeks and finally drained down into the waiting pillow to be sucked and adsorbed into obscurity.

The door creaked and there was a draught of air. Somebody was coming in. It was mother. Juan bit his lips as he managed to smother his sobbing just as mother reached his bed. In one hand she held a tray of containing some vials, cotton and shredding of old clothes. Her other hand was tightly clasped as she swept Juan with a contemptuous glance of unfeeling indifference, a show of insensitivity to which Juan was used to by now. But he knew that in her hearts of hearts she was worried about all of them.

Presently her rotund fist unclasped as she extended his arm in space to grasp the sheet that covered him. With an air of apparent nonchalance she undraped him. Juan was jolted into the realization of his stark nudity as the oppressive air made harsh contact with his mangled skin. He made a feeble attempt to cover himself but that brought only fresh throbs of pain and Juan knew better than not to attempt again.

Lessons of life were conveyed and impressed the hard way in shanty town.

Presently Mama had put down the tray and her stoical grim countenance hovered over Juan like a massive helicopter hovering over its target area. She uncorked the green vial and poured out copious amounts of an iridescent luminous green ointment into a rag swab clutched solemnly in her hand. She straddled Juan's face using one arm and with the other dabbed his grotesque cheeks with the lotion. An excruciating pain seared through Juan's senses and for the second time in the afternoon his eyelids swelled with tears of torment.

His mother gave him one short contemptuous glance and sniggered in a rather dignified manner. Then she went back to the lotion. Juan was always rather perplexed and a bit amused at his mother's dual personality, her ability to lead two different lives. When Pedro was at home she would don the garb of the resolute, stoical, down to earth, insensitive, nihilist iron lady. But once Pedro went out in his routine absences she would at once be reduced to a whimpering, covering coward, pleading for deliverance at the altar of the Almighty.

Whimpering under his breath, tears streaming out of his abused eyes, he tried to peer at his body. The anterior end stretched before him, like a virgin expanse of un-ravaged nature. Sprawling mounds of flesh punctuated by scars, joints and ridges and a prominence surrounded by a black thick undergrowth along the anterior median.

In midst of this rugged terrain, stood an oasis of revolt. An island of mangled torn, offended flesh, an enclave of bruised violated skin, an affidavit to the violence inflicted upon it, offset by a central core of bluish black epicenter where bilirubin had accumulated to ease out the travails of transgressed destitute flesh. It was a mosaic of nearly concentric annuli of shades and hues that vied with and hustled each other to gain prominence and recognition. In close proximity to the central zone was a clear cut ring of deep purple. Beyond it were successive diffused rings of violet, magenta pink and the island was fringed with a dashing tiara of sanguine scarlet. To top it all there was an oleaginous mass oozing out from the central zone where inflammation was progressing.

The sanguine fringe disturbed him greatly and seemed to ring a bell somewhere in same deep crevice of his mind.

"Yes, this color, it was same as that of the outer wound....... the outer wound........ outer wound of father. He had it in his head below his temple, where mother used to kiss him. He was dead then. Then I didn't know. Dear father, poor father, father......."

His thoughts reached a feverish pitch and there was a subdued emotional turbulence in him that drained in his sensitivity and made him inert to the trauma of the ointment treatment.

"Yes Father, I remember him quite clearly now". He thought on, as super fast trains of unrestrained thoughts galloped in his brains. He always had a good memory.

But here also he was at a loss to know what to do with it.

He remembered clearly about the days when father was alive.

It was as though the wound had activated some remote control in his body that released a deluge from his memory data bank. The walls were whiter then and the lawns were greener. Only a faint recollection of sister, but the omnipresent mother was as present then as she is now. Of course she was much more of a handsome lady then and she seemed to bloom and blossom day by day. She had those wonderful dimples on her rusty rose cheeks that measured the degree of her mirth with their depth. Her eyes were rounder and livelier then, two animated bulbs of the pulse of life, two beacons of reassurance and fortitude for the tired and weary.

The dimples had weathered now with the erosion inflicted by time and had become foreboding pits. The eyes were now a frightening, outlandish conglomeration of cataract and painful nostalgia. But curiously enough the strength and reassurance that radiated from her face was potent and virile even now. A fragile compensation for a terrible wreck.

And yes, Pedro was there. His skin was fresher then, though he was very awkward. His gait was unsteady, his talk joyous, and smile impish. He did not have all the foliage and the short growth that he had now on his face. And he went to school. A decent though not very fancied school. Juan also had been promised a future there by his father.

And of course there were those periodical exits of father which used to paralyze the family, as Pedro's did now. It used to puzzle him then. It puzzled him now. It was as if life was a Bioscope and life had realigned itself on reel one. The nerve-wracking tension and high drama enacted out in the house by Pedro and his truant ways was almost an exact re-run of the scenes enacted out by his father and family. Only the characters were different. The basic theme and central plot of the play remained the same.

The deep, somber, phlegmatic clink of a tumbler carrying fluid awakened him from his reverie.

"Milk. Have a nice long drink. Drink it while you still can. We don't have much keep. You need to be strong".

"Yes Ma, I know"

"Don't drink too fast, bad for health"

"Yes Ma, I know"

"Ma, now my cut hurts less, In the face, it is bad but not so in ears............"

His eyeballs lurched sideways as he tried to track his mothers hulk. All it met was the pragmatic, uncompromising sterility of the back of her petticoat. His mother had turned her back. She didn't bother to hear what he had to say. She never really bothered about what, where, how when etc. etc.. At least she pretended so. He enjoyed a kind of freedom that was both pragmatic as well as detrimental.

Prehensile fingers clutched around the glass. One of the brighter aspects of being ill in shantytown was the availability of luxuries like sweetened milk in all abundance and goodness.

⟵◆⟶

Father....... He was really taken aback by the stillness of his father when he had been brought to the house. He fumbled and brooded over the coldness of his usually warm forehead, the curious hole in his temple. It somehow, resembled the holes in their backyard wall where Father had honed and whetted his shooting skills. He also had seen a photograph of father sleeping in a busy public intersection lying flat on his back, surrounded by bawling and animated looking people and flanked by a prostrate bike which also had insisted on sleeping with him. He had wondered as to why of all places, Father had chosen this filthy overcrowded place to sleep. He had also wondered as to how he could manage to shut his eyes and be oblivious of all the pandemonium, hullabaloo and hurly burly around. Their intersection, Gallopade Square, though usually a deserted ghost square, now had become a nerve centre of Medellin momentarily.

Father, as he remembered him had been a great shot and man of few words. He distinctly remembered how he had once shot an apple out of Uncle Marquise's hand and Aunt Marie had fainted.

Father used to say," ***Christ is one, Christ is the truth. He is the essence of life. We are mere bullets fired by him and our aim is to hit the Target as per his wishes. Our destiny and direction is controlled by his aim and he presses the trigger".***

But the same time he also used revile Christ for making the world a one in a million world.

He despised and loathed heaven for making some people rich and some people poor and castigated heaven and its occupants in the most vilifying manner for all the evil omnipresent in the world.

'Conflict of Emotions, intellectual conflict' thought Juan. He had read these words somewhere in a similar context. He knew that he was too young to use such words and logically analyze things as he had done now. People would dismiss him as precocious and say "his prick overgrows his underwear".

But he always knew more than what he was supposed to. He knew what was sex. He had seen people doing it. He knew exactly where 'the thing' went and how 'the thing' functioned.

It had been loquacious, eloquent and articulate love making all the way, when Pedro and Arantxa had coupled. He had screamed 'My Lord, can't wait, can't wait'. She had expostulated 'Slowly, Slowly, Now! Now!' and so an as her supine curvaceous body rocked and swayed in a writhing ballet of frenzied orgy under Pedro's. The cavort-ions and contortions had intensified into a crescendo of frantic hectic movement and there was a flood of effort from Pedro. There were tears and sweat. And then came the absolute stillness.

He did not know how it felt, what were its repercussions and ramifications, but he knew for certain that for one thing it made people blind.

He had craftily closed in for a first hard appraisal of the event when suddenly his eyes met Arantxa's .... moist, lachrymal ones staring into space. Her eyes had met his but there was not a glimmer of recognition or a flick of embarrassment. She just closed her wet eyes and went on.

He also knew it made people happy. He had heard Arantxa laugh shrill, high-pitched, piercing, insinuating peals of gilt edged mirth. The laughter had penetrated his ears, wrought havoc on his nerves and was ensconced in his brain. The very recollection of the event sparked off an uncontrollable throbbing of a vein in his temple. His face moistened and lips grew parched. There was an involuntary, compelling jerking of his loins, a spasmodic, swaying motion which he could not control. But the throbs were uncertain, and the swaying lacked purpose. Soon they subsided.

Young Juan never could really outline his ambitions. But one path stood clear and straight before him. He wanted to make a girl laugh like Arantxa had done.

'But who?, Many ones are there in neighborhood. Grubby petite ones. They never quick lacked the enticement of braids, trinkets and other customary finery'.

He had also caught some interested glances. 'But who perhaps some-one, some-day'.

Chapter 4

The red and white Turbo Harley 350 cc graced the causeway majestically as the morning mist rebounded off its gleaming countenance in patterns of the rainbow. The chirping birds, the somnambulating lizard, and everybody else pranced around it, admiring the mean, tough super-machine.

Then there was a creak, and a flurry of activity that sent the insects and birds scampering off to safer regions. The Master of the Machine trudged out with an assortment of cans and aerosol sprays in his hand. Majestic, indeed, was he, in his liveried mackintosh leather hoses, belted moccasin's and a Crenz Avaro Super Crash Helmet with a retractable VAX- Cramer Polaroid adjustable Visor.

Pedro set down the cans beside his pet with a loud clang and proceeded to make love to his machine as he satiated her lust and longing for grease, engine oil, lubricants and anti-corrosion varnishes.

Juan stepped out of the trellised doorway of his shanty and froze in his steps. Then he stirred and stretched, trying to coax and cajole away the lethargy that had accumulated from the night slumber. He paused and gave a satisfied looking smile as he visualized how he would look in his gleaming polished brand new Crenz Avaro Super Mini

Crash which he now lovingly cradled and caressed in his arm. Arching his spine back on the gnarled stake of their dilapidated fence, he reflected on the turn and twist of events that had led to the present occasion.

He had been standing before the mirror, and had been watering and darkening his would be petunias for some time when Pedro had suddenly and stealthily sneaked upon him. Moustache was too early for him at 10, but so were many other things. Pedro immobilized Juan's face with his vice like grip and gave it a violent twist that made him squeak and execute an about turn. He slapped him hard and as the impact area turned several shades of crimson, he examined the fine piliferous growth encompassing Juan's upper lip.

"Pants down; man"

"Why brother, I not know – why brother?".

"Want more" the hard, shard surfaced palm sliced open the air in its front with a menacing swish.

"Yes I do as you say, no more brother, no more".

"You better do so."

Juan's stuttering hands frantically clutched his zip, which seemed to be held in place by a mammoth magnet.

"Be Fast, you lazy bone"

"Yes brother"

The warning provided the necessary impetus to the faltering hand and the pantaloons slid down Juan's slender legs and folded into two amorphous heaps below him, interlinked by a bridge of rumpled, darned fabric.

"Step out, Fast, Don't stand there staring at me"

"Yes Brother'

Juan made a movement to free himself but one leg seemed to get stuck in one of the hoses.

"Damn, you clumsy oaf"

Before Pedro could comment further, Juan had gained independence.

Pedro bent down and stared right at his manhood. Juan felt like a slave being graded by an appraising glare of a potential customer and went numb with revolt and shame. Pedro Examined the hairy zone, the stubbly bristling posterior zone of younger hairs and the frizzy mature anterior zone where the mature hair had curled over one another for comfort.

Pedro straightened like a lever.

"You wait here, no moving, just wait here".

"I dare not disobey"

"I knew you knew, Now silence".

Pedro retraced his steps to a squalid, dark, grubby coring of the shanty and praised open a wooden chest with a resounding thud. There was a rustling shuffling hiss as he rummaged through its contents.

Presently Pedro was back. His large grasp cornered in its grip a large rolled laminated sheet. Pedro came straight to Juan and stood up straight in his front, his vice like gaze locking Juan.

"Now stare straight, hard what do you see?"

Saying this, with feline agility, he shook open the poster he was holding and a glorious resplendent vision of sexual titillation and concupiscence blasted right into Juan's gaze.

There she lay, on sensuously crumpled satin sheets covered with nothing but a sheer sequined nothing. Trusses of golden fluidity cascaded down her shapely shoulder and merged into the luminescent backdrop. Her face was perfectly chiseled, eyes moist, nose straight and thick sensuous lips parted in a dreamy wistful smile. Her slender long neck led to an enormously buxom bust line. Her svelte waist was stressed by a delicate pink navel. Then the sheer nothings spreading over the sheet did a u-turn and came back to cover a wee bit of the frizz in her loins.

The nothing was there more to accentuate the frizz and the faintly outlined organs rather than to cover it.

Juan knew what it was. His sensibilities were knocked out and he felt himself mature and harden. He looked down and saw his bulbous headed pride stretch straight into the space before it, hard as a bullet. There was curious exhilarating pleasurable pain and Juan's buttocks rocked involuntarily. The reverie was broken by the tearing impact of Pedro's hand on his buttock.

"You are a Man now. Too Early, but yes a Man. Perhaps you will be better than me".

"Yes brother, I'll try".

"A man now, so you should soon learn what men do. I think you know".

"I think so Brother".

"You will soon know more than what you do. You will soon know where I go"

"I'd sure like to Brother".

"Now shut up, and cover yourself, your thing is pretty ugly".

"Yes brother"

Chapter 5

Pedro pressed the throttle and the powerful machine shuddered and thundered as it strived for traction on the brazen asphalt. They were on the main road now and the machine roared on, the pace becoming more scorching to the second. Juan saw the intermittent white strips adorning the mid-centre of the asphalt coalesce into one single straight white stretch.

Suddenly, from far away the wind brought in an unwelcome sound. A slow dull threnody, the sepulchral ululation of the police siren. Juan lurched forward and felt Pedro's rigid back intrude into his belly, suffocate him as the machine decelerated and then dived straight into a side lane. A frantic paced harrowing drive on the narrow flank road, and they were back on the mains.

"Damn foolish, the Police, they always tell you they are coming. Not want them to know where we are going. Not want anyone to know, understand". Pedro muttered through clenched teeth.

"Yes Brother", came the equally gruff response.

Juan knew they were close to the destination. After a bumpy, bone jarring drive on a cobbled, gravelly dirt track through the woods the bike was slowing. Sure enough at a distance, Juan could see a clearing, and a flurry of movement, as humanoid forms scurried to and fro.

There was a screeching lurch as the machine gave a deep mournful squeal as though protesting at the reins being drawn upon its unbridled brute power. The bike slid to a stop and both Juan and Pedro alighted. Pedro adroitly placed the massive hulk into an equilibrium position with a deft kick at the stand. Then he removed his Crenz Avaro and smiled at the gathering.

The clearing was surrounded on three sides by dense, forbidding, impregnable tropical dense evergreens. On the other side, it was guarded by a steep, rocky, solid, weather beaten precipice dotted superficially with blobs and patches of bottle green lichenous and mossy growths. The pinnacle areas were adorned with isolated nests of the magnificent Condor. Below a jutting cornice was a curious pile of conglomerated gravel and pumice. Juan could not figure what it could be.

His attention was now diverted to the populace present, and what a magnificent congregation it was. There were bare chests, glistening leather skin tights, long shaggy trusses, permanent stubbles, each member vying to be as much a likening of Carlos as he could be. These people would have resorted to plastic surgery if it were within their reach and means. Their bodies were resplendent with steamy glistening sweat. Precipitated slightly away from the congregation of men, was a small group of animated sprightly young girls, all in crash outfits. Beside them was an array of gleaming Harley Davidsons and Turbo Max- wells. Juan could not comprehend; try as he might, the purpose and the nature of their presence.

The murmur was sliced open with a whip-crack sound of a pistol being fired into the air. A hush descended. Then there was a flurry of movement as men slid into a regulated formation. Another hush.

A band struck up a lively tune. And soon the mass of humanity conglomerated into one rhythm of disciplined, orchestrated, choreographed movements. Beads of sweat adorned the dazzling foreheads of the young men as the muscles strained and hearts pumped. It was drill-time in the right earnest.

The end of the drill was followed by a short break where the young recuperated and rejuvenated their flagging stamina and morale. Soon they were lining up into batches of ten. Juan could count at least nine batches, bunches of tired but determined, resolute men, banking on some inexhaustible, effulgent geyser of energy.

Another crack and one batch of men had lined up at a point marked by a painted jutting rod. The men crouched and assumed the classic athletic stance. Legs were coiled and arms bent, a potent source of potential energy waiting for release. A Burly man with a timer assumed his place near another rod and presumably the finish. From the apparent distance between the rods Juan could say that the distance was 100 meters. At some distance stood a rather mean looking hawk-like man, impeccably dressed in tweed, his bowler's hat tipped jauntily to one end. He had a quite domineering and self-important air around him from which Juan could say that for the moment, he was the man at the helm.

Another crack and the men were off, a throbbing multitude of flailing arms, thumping legs, pumping hearts and lots and lots of adrenalin.

"All below 11", the burly man at finish shouted.

"Are you sure, double check fast?"

It was the hawk.

"Yes sir, no problems, timer checked ten times before the trial"

"Okay well done, it's quite satisfactory"

"Thank you sir"

"Now girls, it's your turn to do your bit for your Godfather. Now serve these tired bulls well. No-one leaves here with an inch of empty space in his belly. Nobody grudges refreshing treatment for deserving people. Yes?"

"Yes Sir", high pitchy voices chorused. A motor roared into life and a diminutive car hauled up a pantry car into view from the nearby under growth. The girls lined up and the pulse of activity began in the fullness.

Soon copious quantities of grilled spiced beef, ham, lard, sour cheese and cans of root beer were passed around and the batch sat down at a satisfying round of delicatessen.

Meanwhile more batches lined up and had their go. The burly man shouted himself hoarse.

The last batch assumed their position at the start marker of their ordeal. The air had a relaxed fragrance and tension was low. Almost all had qualified and this was the last batch. The whip crack of the pistol ignited the fuse of unbounded energy and dust rose once again from the over used tracks.

———◆———

Andreas had been physically and emotionally drained and depleted by a devastating bout of influenza. But he had come, because he knew what the consequences would be, if he did not turn up after receiving the Godfather's summons.

It had been a tenacious battle against a debilitating, overwhelming fatigue all through the exercise regimen. He had a funny vacuous feeling in his abdomen and felt ants crawling in his veins and entrails. His senses would intermittently and individually blot out. Sometimes he found himself staring into an impervious white blanked screen with blinking phosphorescence, and sometimes his ears would become inert to his environment and the only audio impulse registered was a dull buzzing ringing sound.

The recuperation time was to be utilized hundred percent and so was the case. Andreas did a number of relaxation and rejuvenation exercises and tried to psyche himself up by concentrating.

He knew that the battle was over even before it was fought.

"I know I am finished. But fight I must".

He crouched low at the start, tensed and turgid trying to conjure out some impetus from his fatigued, flagging, flaccid muscles.

The first 50 meters came off without a hitch. Andreas' determination and grit seemed to have won him the battle. Then suddenly, his heel failed him. His left foot seemed to turn to jelly and his muscles pliant. He made one massive effort to launch himself into another awesome stride. But the house of cards had come down. He collapsed into a numb, writhing mass in the middle of the wake of dust left by other runners.

Juan had been watching the races with unfailing inexorable relish. The last race had about as much charm for him as the first one. The stereotyped start was followed by a flurry of activity as usual. But suddenly, near the half way mark, one runner just tumbled down.

"As to what happened?, he has collapsed as though he is axed down".

The man who was down, thrashed about, and then became still.

"Dead?."

Suddenly the runner's feet and hand lived, and they curled up. They slowly arched themselves into a mesh like formation, as though trying to cover and armor the vulnerable constituents of the body.

Sure enough the Hectors closed in upon him. Juan knew what was going to happen. All know what was going to happen. The air was heavy with a chari-vari that seemed to come from everywhere. The murmur died down as the circle tightened as was replaced by the even more oppressive and ominous silence.

All at once, Andreas was pummeled from all sides with a rain of full blooded kicks. He tried in vain to fend off the blows. But soon lights blotted out. But the clobbering continued as the Hench men, addicted to sadistic glee, frenzied in an orgy of violent cruelty. The limp body was tossed to and fro as blows-were directed at it, from all possible angles.

The roar of a mean machine sliced open the commotion and the crowd cleared. It was Arantxa on a blue-black

Harley complete in crash regalia. The limp body was lifted and strapped at the back with leather belts.

"Dump him in his backyard, the bastard. Let his mum see her fucks consequence". It was the man in tweeds.

Arantxa roared off dutifully.

Soon the air was rent with an ear splitting roar, the thrashing sound of giant propeller fans tearing apart the turbulent atmosphere.

"Godfather" said Pedro.

Juan forgot to blink.

The giant mechanical bird hovered about the congregation, like a magnificent condor balancing itself in midflight before taking the dive of fruition. Soon enough the plunge was executed.

Chapter 6

The helicopter descended and climbed down the echelons of altitude at a steady pace and finally ensconced itself into the hoary blinding whirl pool of loose dust scattered in its wake. The raucous expostulations of the machine smothered and stifled, as the motor was shut off. It stood steady in its place emitting a steady dying clackety-clack. Soon the sibilant machine-bird was still.

Still enough......., for the bulbous, tinted, triplex doors to swing open. Juan could recognize a Seville Row from 100 yards. After all Carlos had worn them as his trademark for nearly 6 years. The man in Seville Row stepped out. His small weasel like face was half blotted, by rather oversized Aviator Sunglasses. His aquiline nose probed into the environment, as though trying to sniff out the situation.

He stepped down.

"What a paunch! Larger than my pillow and bedding put together" thought Juan.

A man with a loud speaker slung along his left shoulder made bee-line for the copter and screeched to a halt before it.

Heels clicked. It was followed by a crisp smart salute.

"Everything okay I hope".

"Yes, Sir. Miguel manages fine".

The index finger pointed at the Man in Tweeds.

The Godfathers swept Miguel off his feet with an endearing look.

"Deserving men never go unrewarded by the Cartel. It is not like our country, the administration and government, where everything goes by bribe and back door. Here at the Cartel, merit comes first."

Miguel beamed, and Juan could perceive the radiance emanating from his countenance from fifty yards.

The Seville Row adorned arm beckoned the man with the loudspeaker. Godfather took the microphone in his hands and blew into it. There was a sharp wheezing exacerbating sound. Everything was fine. They had to be with the Cartel. The address began.

"Brothers, Sisters and Fellow Fraternity of the one and only Great Family. You can well imagine and contemplate the profound happiness and consuming mirth, that I am experiencing upon seeing you all here together as dedicated diligent servants of the Cartel, as we all are. The Family, that is we, mind you each person present here is a good and equal part of the Family, is indeed proud and happy, justifiably, at your commendable and exemplary service."

"Some parity, Bloody Fucker!!! Parity it is, that is we get. Bullets for us and for you the play-mates for yar loins. Base fooling". Pedro could not help sighing inspite of himself.

"Any thing wrong?"

"Nothing Pal, Hear. Hear what the boss has to say".

"We all know that the Cartel is much more creditable and reliable than the bloody government that rules here. The Cartel takes care of those who serve it. And mighty well, at that. But in Government, masses bleed while

officers stash away the cash. You will all be glad to know that some embodiments of superhuman courage have chosen this fine day to display their supreme sense of sacrifice, for the family, and for consummate dexterity and adroitness with their job. This will pave the way, for their aggrandizement and fruition. I'd not like to waste any more time. Let the big test begin. And may Almighty bless and fortify all those who are taking the ordeal. There will be two minutes of silence in remembrance of JESUS Christ, when all present will pray for the successful Emergence of all those who take part in this final test and then we will begin the occasion. Praised be the Lord, Hallelujah .... Amen."

A dutiful cross by all, and then silence.

Pedro grasped Juan by collar and yanked him off the ground. A startled Juan stumbled and then steadied himself.

"Cross yourselves brother, today we make it or break it."

"But what's happening. Where do I break or make. What do I make?"

A cloud of somber solemnity swept and enshrouded Pedro's face. He opened his mouth to say something, but then swallowed. Juan had never seen Pedro's Adams apple stand out so prominently. Pedro tightened his grip on Juan's shoulder, and he almost gasped due to suffocation. Pedro was clearly in torment. He was making a gallant effort to open his heart.

"Juan my boy! I'm going to shoot an apple placed in your head"

Juan went limp in Pedro's hand and his knees wobbled.

'Don't worry my dear brother, don't worry. You don't trust me? You don't trust my aim? Don't we need more money? Don't Juanita want to marry? Doesn't our mother like to have a servant? Please don't be afraid. Please???" Juan looked into his brothers eyes and shuddered involuntarily.

"Don't worry brother. I swear by Christ that if I harm you. I'll never spare myself. You believe in Christ? Don't you? I have seen you cry in Church. Have Faith in him please. For mum's sake."

Pistols and apples were being handed out. Pedro tugged Juan. He thought of mother swallowed by her tedious drudgery. He thought of pretty Juanita. Suddenly strength returned to Juan's knees and he walked again.

Five boys stood in the harsh sunlight eyes closed, apples on head and prayers on their mouths. At 50 yards away to them, stood five young men in their early teens, each ones hand clasping a Colt Automatic 0.22. Ominous stiffness bore heavy and people started sweat without reason. The enormity and character of the occasion seemed to have impressed upon all animate dwellers in the proximity. Even the birds were silent. ***Fate was at hand.***

The muzzles of the Colt Automatics drew parallel to the ground. Eyes narrowed. Brows sweated. Forefinger curled around triggers waiting to release destiny. Mouths went dry. Juan stared straight ahead.

"Christ give me strength. I am not afraid to die. Die I may. But die I will for my mother. My father's died. Mother will die. I shall die one day. May be today. So what?"

He blinked his eyes. Upon reopening them he found himself looking straight into the muzzle of the colt automatic cradled in Pedro's arm. For the second time in the day, fear and foreboding overwhelmed him. He wanted to run away. But the legs would not respond to the command. They froze.

Cold sweat trickled down his forehead and got into his eyes.
They burned furiously. He tried to close them. But could
not. Now he stared into a blankness that made its sudden
appearance before him, oblivious of the burning in his eyes
and waited.

The crack came. And ears exploded and revolted at the
roar of thunderclaps. Then they went haywire. Juan fell
down prostrate on the ground. He waited with bated breath
and clenched teeth, for the searing, nerve blasting pain,
that would rape and ravish his senses before snuffing life
out of his mangled body. But there was none. Soon senses
dawned. He became faintly aware of ambrosia of sticky,
sweet, smelling sap running down his forehead. He waited
for the hot spouting blood. But there was only the mashed
pulp and mangled rind. A strong arm slipped around him,
and Juan was heaved from ground and was precipitated
against the broad chest of Pedro.

"We did it brother, yes we did it. We'll be rich, we'll
have house, nice homes, Mum will have maid, you will have
bike, we did it, Christ helped us. Lord be praised".

Juan snuggled and burrowed deeper into the artificial
leather on Pedro's chest.

'Yes we did it:' he thought, 'we did it, I too did it.'

He was happy. His, being was of consequence and his
Existence had served some purpose.

'Ye we did it' Juan murmured in hushed tones.

———◈———

Hands curling around trigging tightened. Then came
the deafening roar. All closed their eyes involuntarily. Then
eyes flicked open. There was pulp on the head of the first

boy. Rind on the head on second boy. But blood spewed out of a hole, in the head of the third. The boy staggered and then collapsed into a witling, arching, heap going through death throes. The body lay flat on the ground like a mulberry tree axed by an invisible tomahawk.

Another thunderous bang sent the birds screaming and screeching into the air. The boy's brother, the shooter, too lay crumpled in a heap, blood staining the ground around his right temple crimson. The two oases of blood glinted in the bright sun. The wind went on its way. Sun battered on in a bid to shrivel up the murdered bodies.

Chapter 7

"Juan, Hurry up, come here".

"Yes Brother, coming."

"If you knew, what I have for you, you would bolt here."

Juan broke into a fast trot, and screeched to a somewhat undignified stop in front of his brother seated on an army chair.

"Rather like a tricycle' thought Juan disgustedly, "my skates are as exciting as a snail."

"What is it brother?".

The right of hand of Pedro made a frantic dive towards his pocket, and soon it was in possession of a luxuriously wrapped caramel bar.

"Wow brother! Thanks you."

"All yours"

As Juan unwrapped the treasure, his mind went into fifth gear. Caramel bars, were not common property in shantytown. They always served some purpose.

"It is to cool your nerves. If they are tight, that is".

It seemed that through some invisible extra sensory perception, his brother could read his mind like a newspaper.

"What for?"

"So you do want to know."

A cloud came over Pedro's face. Never before had it appeared so grizzly and so stubbly is it was now to Juan.

"You have always wanted to know where I go when hell breaks loose in the house. Don't you? So now get ready to hear it. Well, ...I, I go out on my Contract. Contract to kill. Kill people, live people. People who move. I kill to live, that's what we do, and that's what your father did. That's what you will do too.

Like The deserts of Andes, or forests of Amazon. Kill or die. Kill to stay alive. There is no other way. It's the only door open for a shantytown child who wants to live. You have to kill to live. We have to kill to stay alive. No other door."

"Oh Christ!. How could you....". Juan forgot to chew the caramel that had got stuck in between his teeth. Willies were playing all over his nerves and his confidence melted like snow swallowed by live charcoal.

"Forget Christ. Forget him and You, You Open your Ears and listen what I am saying".

Juan was feeling too faint to reply. But his senses were well oiled and were prepared to meet the situation. He decided to listen and keep quiet.

"Now let me tell you this, your father killed to live and got killed. I kill to live and will get killed. Then you are next. So be prepared."

Juan was fighting severe asphyxia and a blaze seemed to have enveloped his cerebrum.

"You see we are all instruments the hand of the masters when we kill. We are only the instrument. The instrument is not to blame. You have to realize this,

and also that we are all instruments in the hands of our ultimate master."

"When knife pierces heart, people get killed, and not the knife, understand".

Juan found words flooding his tongue at last.

"But brother, let me tell you one thing. I am a child of Christ, and children of Christ don't kill other".

"Fuck your Fuck-stick, you and your Jeezeses, Fuck your Jesus and ask him why you were born here. Now that you bastard, have invaded our mom's stomach, you'll have to protect it. You fool won't understand as long as ya get grog to eat, and bed to sleep. You know now clear, that all this is because I kill"

There was no reply from Juan's part. Things were being drowned down his ears. Slowly they were taking impact. Pedro was quick to see it.

"It is before your own eyes that I was promoted. Now it is all likeness that we might live in Pensioners Hill and fuck off from this mouse house. But then, it is even more possible that I get killed. What are ya going to do after that? You'll make mother a sweater? So that you get food and bed?"

"I think you are old enough to understand".

"Yes"

The response had pleased Pedro evidently. His features smoothed down and a smile played on his lips.

"You see, you are old enough to understand and you must understand"

Juan looked down at the caramel bar. It had reduced to half its original size and Juan did not know how.

"Let me make one point clear to you. The men we kill are mostly Evil men. The world is evil. Otherwise

it would not have been so uneven. There are haves and there are have-nots. The haves go on having more. All are engaged in constant battle to keep the tummy out and abdomen level. The only difference is that while the rich try to trim down upon the convex, we the poor, try to level up the concave of our stomach. Wealth like wine, is intoxication. The more you have it, the more you need it. The rich men are all a bunch of cut-throats, who can go to any extent. So holing them is not a sin. We are in fact trying to establish parity. We draw the wealth out of rich and use it ourselves. This is no crime, at least in the eyes of God."

Juan nodded. He was beginning to get the hang of it. He had seen the plush mansions at Pensioner's Hill, and what a contrast it was to their humble dwellings.

"Surely this injustice must end. This inequality has to be kicked out". Juan thought, "But to kill for it. I don't know".

"You know Juan. All the problems that we face, unemployment, hunger, disease, dirt. They are all a result of over population. And you know, who are over populating the country. It is those bastards, the rich and powerful. Each bloody fool will have one legal and at least ten illegal wives. His wife will push out ten and each of the concubines will have fifteen. These children live like Gods. They get best of things. And when they become big, they mop up all the jobs. They naturally buy work. So there is nothing honest and straight left for us people. It in fact we'd be dong a service to the fatherland, by eliminating these fucking turncoat pigs."

"But all rich can't be all that bad. Besides there is God."

"They are all bad. Believe me. Their wealth makes them bad. Now listen, Juan, you have to do this, so that at least your grand children may say that there is God. It is your duty to them. You have to do this job not so that at least they get a chance to be honest and straight. Don't you feel you owe it to them?"

"I guess so".

"If you are afraid, then you should not do this job. Better let mum suck when I am gone. But if you wanna be a man, you gotta do it. You want to be a man?"

Juan looked Pedro straight in the eye. His Adam's apple protruded as he strained for articulation. Even Pedro was taken aback by Juan's look and he blinked.

"Yes I want to be a man, I wanna do things men do. I wanna be like you brother, I wanna be like you."

The last pocket of resistance of the caramel bar slid down Juan's grasp, and fell with a soft thud. Juan lifted his feet, and resolutely stamped it into pulp. Pedro smiled.

Morning sun stared into Juan's face coming right at him along the cobbled walk way. There were no sudden spurts of speed, no balancing tricks, no meandering, no beer cans. Just plain healthy, long, puffing strides.

Juan had decided that he would take a plain fast run one day, and a dribbling one the next. ***One day he would train to be a killer and the other day to be a footballer.***

'One never know". He thought. Feet picked up hails of assorted gravel as they flailed on.

Chapter 8

The mighty roar of the indignant HARLEY turbo 500 made mockery of the relative calm of the juvenile morning air. Vulcanized rubber skimmed and tore over meticulously leveled concrete. The man in flamboyant red who adorned the magnificent machine looked straight ahead.

"Earlier it was asphalt, Now it is concrete, Earlier one way. Now 4 laned, Next what? Does the world have to change infinitely at this scorching pace?" Juan could not help sighing in spite of himself.

Suddenly the virgin thunder of the Harley Turbo metamorphosed into a discordant trundle. There were a few piercing honks. But before Juan could glance up the rear view, a well defined mass of stream-lined red streaked past him.

"Wow, a Ferrari Sports, Don't see many of them around. Lucky chap", thought Juan.

But at that instant a mane of red hair caught his eye.

To be beaten by an aristocrat, that too by a measly woman, was too much for the fired up blood of the now angry and young, and all of eighteen, Juan.

Fifth gear and full throttle came next.

The gap between the car and the bike at first curtailed, and then steadied. The car clearly was of plutocratic origin. The red glazing surface translated the young sun into multitudes of iridescent hues.

"Bloody Slovenly Trollop", thought Juan and he exhausted his biceps as the accelerator trying to spur on his machine to consummate performance. The machine exploded into a deafening earth shaking rumpus and rushed forth like a mad bull.

The 7th Declivity was approaching.

"She'll have to slow here, my bike doesn't have to. That is where I overtake" thought Juan and accelerated on now with patience. The turn was to the right and the bike lane being to the left had a much larger detour and hence a larger arc of greater radius. Therefore the centrifugal force would be less and the bikes need not to slow down.

The declivity approached. But suddenly, the bandana adorning the girls neck unwrapped itself and came straight at Juan. He tried to avoid it but it was too late.

The bandana at first caressed, and then incarcerated Juan's eyes in a maddening embrace of stone blindness. Juan braked frantically. The vulcanized rubber at first waltzed with the concrete, before finally resolutely precipitating itself against it, with a resounding thud. Juan plummeted through the still air and landed flat on his back.

"My God, is this apoplexy for rest of my life".

Juan tried to sit up. Miraculously he could.

"Thank God, No damage, Christ be praised".

"Well it was very nice of you to set up this acrobatic show for me".

Juan was surprised by the shrillness of the voice. It seemed to remind him of some body.

"Maybe some dammit child hood memories", thought Juan.

He lifted his eyes. They clashed with the mocking gaze of a young pretty brunette. Juan felt like a discarded cuspidor.

"Hurt?"

"Never."

"Brave young Brutes like you don't get hurt- Especially when a Chick in a Ferrari is moving nearby" the sarcasm in the voice sliced Juan's mind.

His indignation gave way to irritation.

"You low life street walker, if you hadn't thrown your bandanna at me, I'd have shut your mouth and ya'r engine at the same time. Cheat! Tricking me off and then gloating. Miserable."

"Take it easy, young man, take it easy. You needn't hot up so much. By the way is this the way you talk to a lady. Where are your etiquette and manners?"

"I stuffed them down ya's cunt".

"Very polite, I'd say. But wait a minute. I like it. That is the spirit. By the way how old are ya?"

Juan removed his Crenz Avaro to display his eternal stubble.

"I'm Eighteen, ya know, that is young enough to rape ya, Do you understand".

"Perfectly, You a virgin?"

"Ya, Bet".

"I don't believe you????"

"You don't have to. I don't care"

"Nor do I. It's fine. It'll be fun"

"What'll be fun"

"Never mind. First stop being a virgin. Then ya'll understand"

"Well, I'd say….."

"Where do you live by the way?"

"Pensioners Hill. Fourth bungalow on the Vinci street".

"Pretty posh place that is".

"If you say so. But where do you live?"

"Goth Heights".

"My word! You in elite. Where you and where I. I'm not that respectable? I should confess".

"Neither are we. Ya know, they say Earth revolves around sun. But I say it revolves around money. Mind you. Money made shamelessly will remove the shame incurred in making it".

"I guess so". Juan was beginning to feel a bit uncomfortable and restive.

"So you don't believe me", the girl had noticed the cloud on Juan's face. "It's all generation gap. You are 18 and I am 20. 2 years is a gap nowadays. When you are twenty you will understand you know. It is funny how we change with time.

When we are two there are no flaws. First lies come out then we are three. And by the time we are twenty, all are whores. Well almost all are".

"You got a point there"

Vera giggled and looked at Juan slyly." I wish had your point here". And she shamelessly pointed towards her crotch.

Then her hand went down and gave a soft erotic massage to the area for an instant.

Never before had Juan encountered such flagrantly scandalous and shameless behavior. He went red in the face and fumbled for words. Instinct told him to throttle off. But some mysterious enigmatic force was holding him back. His mind raced for something to say.

"Your name please". Finally he blurted out.

"Vera D. Costa. Father is Alexander D Costa. He is a judge."

"I have heard his name. Pedro, my brother, says that he is intelligent and will live long. He also says that his co-operation will win him money. Lots of it."

"Yes he is indeed quite sensible. He knows that self comes before duty and it is not the other way round"

"Like father, like daughter." Juan could not help musing to himself.

"You said something?" Vera interjected.

"Will you come over to my place someday?"

"I'll be glad to".

"Of course, I am not in a position to formally invite you, as you people usually do".

"Oh, leave it, I don't believe in any bloody formalities. In fact I don't believe in anything".

She smiled sweetly at Juan.

And he felt his stomach blow in.

"By the way, where did you say you lived?"

"I said before, fourth bungalow, Vinci street…."

"Pensioners Hill, I know."

Chapter 9

"The meal was good". Vera sank lazily into the satin sofa.

"They always are, at the Rodeos. That is why I took you there".

"Now we have the whole evening before us, nothing to do. Let us go over to your place".

"But it is far from Goth heights. Besides Pedro, mum and Juanita are out to visit an aunt".

"That makes things simpler. Now speed off. Destination Pensioner's Hill".

"As you say".

Pedro grappled with throttle and the Turbo displayed what it could do.

"Smart place. As smart inside as outside".

Vera sprawled herself upon the richly veloured sofa and purred with feline intimacy.

"We should make good use of the time we get together. And alone at that".

"I guess so". Juan was feeling hot in his neck and his hair bristled with excitement.

Involuntarily he sat down beside Vera. His manhood was now straining against his underpants and he was painfully aware of this.

Vera gave a little laugh and arched herself up so that her full breasts pressed firmly into Juan's face. Juan felt like tearing loose but he could not. He found himself burying his face into the cleavage in between her ripe nipples. A sob broke out from his throat. Hot tears rolled down his cheeks and flooded the valley in between Vera's breasts.

Suddenly Vera's hand shot down and caught hold of the satin of her dress. Then in a slow sensual motion she began drawing it up. Juan stared though misted eyes, as inch after inch of shapely flesh unfolded before his steamy gaze. Vera pushed the skirt up enough for him to see that she wore nothing inside. He stared at the faint frizzy that was visible and felt his lips go dry. He stared at her thighs and crotch that were clearly visible. Then Vera's hand came over the crotch and massaged it gently. Her lips pressed against Juan's. Her tongue invaded Juan's mouth and Juan was on fire. He slid back and lay flat on his spine. Vera straddled him with one leg and then moved forward so that she was directly over Juan's face. She swept aside the frock and pressed her pubis against Juan's face. It was bristly and wet.

"Kiss me" she said.

Try as he did not to, he found himself burying his nose into the ravine flanked by undergrowth. A gummy sweet smelling fluid oozed out from the ravine. It was on high tide. The fluid blended with Juan's tears and drained down slowly from his face.

Then Vera drew back and unbuttoned his pants and zipped open his underpants. His protuberance flew out.

She caressed it with her lips and then rolled her tongue over its base fertilizing it to the core. Then she widened the gap between her legs and placed it firmly where she wanted it to go. Then she laughed. A piercing, squealing, high voltage laughter. It seared down Juan's ears and set his veins on fire. The skin of Juan's temple throbbed and his loins jerked violently. It reminded him of something... some one,..... a faint recollection of some boyhood memory, ensconced in his brain.

"Arantxa", he thought, "she used to laugh like this".

He had at that time wanted to make somebody laugh like her. Vera's laugh was not as shrill or as high-pitched, but it was invigorating and titillating all the same. His loins gave way to an overwhelming spasm of throbbing swaying motion. This time they were not purposeless, as they were 8 years ago.

Chapter 10

The giant crimson ball hanging in vacuum swabbed and swept Pensioner's Hill in a dazzling cascade of sanguine and bountiful rays. Pensioner's Hill glowed and looked like a mammoth infinitesimally pure Ruby dazzling forth its brilliant resplendent arrogance.

Juan returned back from his jog and was surprised to find Pedro leaning at a precarious angle against the quaintly balustraded and majestic porch. His face was affected by a diadem of intertwined intermeshed frowns. The furrows appeared to be deeper than last time. Juan always thought it curious the way the furrows enhanced their relevance with each mission by increasing their depth.

Juan dove through the trellised ornate archway and made bee-line for Pedro.

"Another mission brother?"

Pedro gave a start, as though he had been rudely shaken out from some reverie or séance. Swiftly, with masculine immaculateness, he regained his composure and faced Juan as an Embodiment of dignity.

"Yes" the words sank deep into the air.

"So what is new? There have been many. Why be so pensive about this one?"

"It is much more dangerous than I've ever had. I only hope that I came out unscathed".

"You will, you have done it so many times. Every time you have clicked. So why not now? By the way, will you tell me what all this is about?"

"Let me tell you one thing. One vital component of our trade is not to confide your plans to anybody. Not even to your shadow. And I want this to sink in. You will be assuming charge, in case I am gone this time".

"Come on, Don't be too philosophical. Have faith in God. It's he who decides. We just follow his will".

"Now who is being philosophical?".

Pedro's avuncular tone nearly surprised Juan.

"He's beaming OLD fast". He thought.

Four days had passed since Pedro mounted the white pick-up to bid "A Definitive Adios" to some wretched soul. A delay of this magnitude, was a desultory formality, from the day Pedro set out. The Contract should have been executed the day Pedro set out. The rest of the delay usually incorporated the remuneration formalities and procedures. Their mother was at her supreme loquacity throughout the wait and took the storm in her stride. There was not even a miniature iota of the apprehensive, querulous, unkempt, emancipated whimpering wreck of the destitute past. Nor were there any demented paroxysm of frenzied bedlam from Juanita. It was as though some infallible clairvoyant had confidently prognosed the safe return of Pedro.

'Mother's stoic phlegmatic self had become more resolute with age' thought Juan.

<hr />

The morning paper, immaculately rolled up into a neat roll, plummeted gracefully thorough the air before crashing down into the porch of fourth bungalow, Vinci Street, Pensioner's Hill, with a dull resounding thud. Juan's numb senses ignited into a flurry of unmitigated adrenalin, as he tore to the porch in pursuit of the paper. His anxiety was understandable. After all the morning paper had always been the first to intimate Pedro's family of his Exploits.

"Would be Assassin shot dead by Alert Guards" the brazen headline screamed and blasted straight into Juan's senses and blew his nerves inside out. Cold sweat trickled down his cheeks as he steadied himself and bit his lips in a attempt to regain composure. Eyes scanned and scoured the vituperative parchment for the mug shot. It was Pedro all right, sprawled and frigid in a pool of blood, eyes half open and right temple punctured. He laid there among curious bystanders. Exactly as his father had laid fourteen years back.

A sob broke from Juan's throat as he curled over himself.

———✦◈✦———

Mother and Juanita were in a comatose state. Neighbors had come in to display shadow remorse. The room was stuffy. This coupled with the abundance of crocodile tears in the room stifled Juan and involuntarily he walked out of the room.

The mellowing twilight and a freshening breeze made him feel better once he was outside. He lit a cigarette and browsed over the suddenness of events that preceded this night.

"Two options, two options Man. Either follow suit.
Or use your diploma. Some Gods tell me what to do."

Juan's thoughts were racing at a feverish pitch.

"Yes, third option is available, die myself. What to do?
Father n brother's said to take up their line. But I'm not
sure".

"Give me the answer O Christ, the answer" he
shouted and hammered his hairy chest. The golden cross
strapped to the chain strung around his neck flew out
and executed a brief dazzle in the fading light.

"I got the answer. Thank you, Lord. I got it".

A dim grim smile skimmed across his, rugged stubble
cheek.

Chapter 11

The ornate walls of the bungalow reverberated under the collective impact of five pairs of boots.

"Care for coffee?". Juan was well bred enough to enact his little nuance of curtsy.

"Yes it will do some good", it was the point nosed man in the canary casual. The men plonked themselves upon the lavish velour and mahogany sofa. All were impeccably dressed and well nourished. The huge cavities they created on the sofa bore testimony to their health.

"Coffee was good".

It was the point nosed man again.

Juan looked straight and bemusedly at the angular features. This man meant business, he knew.

"We need no introduction. Nor do you, the brother of the illustrious Pedro, who sacrificed all for the Family."

Juan felt his throat choke and a nerve batted in his eyelid.

The poker nosed man continued his obviously pre-rehearsed speech.

"Your brother must at some juncture or other, appraised you of your duties and obligations in the eventuality of his demise. He must have made you aware

of what you owe to your family and to the Greater Family. And I am sure that a young, dynamic, intelligent young man like you will heed the advice of his experienced brother. What to say something?"

"No comments". Juan's reply given through clenched teeth was terse and brusque. The force of Juan's tame knocked the Poker Nose out of his Elements for a second. This was not quite what he expected. But he regained his composure swiftly.

"It would be my pleasure to inform you that your personal status of being brother of late Pedro exempts you from the rigorous test of skill that you are required to take before being a Class 1. I'm sure that in your long and intimate association with Pedro, you have learnt enough to be a master craftsman. So let me present you with contract."

He stood up with a click and sleightfully pushed his hand to and fro in his coat and hey presto, a laminated sheet of paper materialized in his hand.

"The terms are simple. Number one, The Family looks after your family in case of your demise. Number two, it is either you or the target. There is absolutely no room for mistakes. Number three, if you try to evade the term of five years, get the 'definitive adios'. Now please sign your name here".

"What if I don't" ......the words spat upon the face of the man on Carnaby casual. He staggered under its impact and then steadied himself. The icy glint of his mesmeric steely eyes riveted and ensnared Juan. The thin mouth spat open showing aged gold liveried teeth.

"Nothing, only the Family absolves itself from at any responsibility of you and your family. You are free to look after yourself. The cartel will only be glad to do some service to God by transporting another poor soul from Shantytown to Pensioner's Hill."

"I know what service you do to God. You bastards, you are messengers of Satan". The words came out in short spasmodic gasps. Juan was getting incoherent. He could say no more. With burning fiery eyes Juan pounced upon the contract and held it straight in between him and the agent. Then with one swift motion he tore it into half. The agent's sneering countenance erupted from behind. The smile that was entrenched upon his frozen hair line lips was half quizzical and half prophetical.

Chapter 12

The overwhelming phlegmatic iciness, of the bitter vengeful south wind wrought mayhem to the mutilated mauled oak trees that lined up the Grand Trunk Road. The decapitated stubs on the oaks wept copiously at the natural demises of their protégés with plentiful sap, as the dead leaves surfed through the biting atmosphere like trapeze artistes not able to make up their mind, before laying themselves to rest ungracefully on their overcrowded mass grave, the pavement of Grand Trunk.

Scores of rakes and brooms pricked and abused their corpses and unceremoniously huddled them into demeaning heaps before enacting their last rites by burning them.

The workers who tended these pavements were an overworked, under nourished, famished lot. Chartism to them, was a Non-entity. Day after day, night after night, they watered the desolate gravel with the brine oozing out of their foreheads, so that the wake of limousines of VIPs do not invite an unwelcome shower of dehydrated foliage upon the following cars.

Suddenly a bell rang from no-where. The shift was over. Juan sat among others in the frowzy littered park to gulp down a frugal lunch of salted bread with toasted cheese.

Food went impromptu into the mouth and pabulum into his cerebrum.

He thought of how he was shoved out of a dozen offices where he had approached with a childlike ardor fortified by his diploma in Chemical Engineering. He thought of the rank naked corruption, nepotism and cruelty that he had encountered in his endeavors for a decent job, the curmudgeons who had reviled him, the sequined secretaries who had sneered at him.

He gave a big gasp and started coughing. Some bread had wandered into his trachea. He opened the bottle that lay by his side and tried to alleviate his torments with a few forced gulps of ice-cold water. Above his head, the wind was sibilant and the shower of mottled oak leaves continued to fall upon the mottled souls below like confetti. Some wretched souls curled over one another in an effort to salvage some warmth before some police man ejected them from the park. Nearby a group of sozzled wasted wrecks tried to fill up the vacuum in their lives with more illicit spirits. A constant beat was kept up on old beer cans in an effort to inundate the reality, and for at least a moment, to be happy and comfortable. Some people revisited stale jokes and the audiences stretched their lips in a vain effort to show appreciation. Some had simply forgotten how to laugh and could not even concentrate on the anecdotes.

"At least God gave me a home to go to". Juan could not help thinking. But the thought of home had its ugly manifestations as well. He was reminded of his mother who was breathing her last in a desolate, barren chilly damp room in a stylish bungalow on Pensioner's Hill. His eyes moistened and lips trembled. But no tears came. They eyes has built up an immune system to tears. Otherwise there would be time only for them.

He had pawned off almost all the furniture in a last ditch desperate effort to sustain the last source of affection and understanding that was left for him in the world. The only furniture left in the house was the oak cot on which his mother waited for her tryst with destiny. It was only now when the end was near, that he realized how much his mother mattered to him.

The overworked, heavy, patched scrawny shoes trampled the fallen leaves with some noisy defiance. The crimson ball was half gobbled up by horizon and straying birds were making beeway to their vantage points.

Juan coughed as he tramped along. It was getting late. He decided to take the Link Road via Hotel May Fair. He was fully aware of the notoriety of Ninth Link Road and Hotel May Fair. It was a shadowy refuge of prostitutes of all echelons and denominations. The High Society Call Girls inundated their concavities caressed by the sensual effulgence of satin and foam in the luxury suites of May Fair. The second grade whores frequented nearby bistros in search of the debauches. The lowest category did the needful on the streets, nooks and corners, where streetlights were killed off. Ninth link road was the nucleus of Medellin's hedonistic profanity and lasciviousness.

Juan quickened his pace. The ladies of the night were there all right, wearing all sorts of vinyl nothings. The dresses were strategically split, at vital locations, to expose tantalizing morsels of titillating pubic hair, cleavage or ripe nipples. All masculine passers were greeted with a chorus of giggles and provocative gestures. Juan stared straight ahead and walked mumbling Christ. But then a flicker of stealthy movement caught his eye. He turned just in time to catch a fleeting glimpse of her. A mane of brown hair was disappearing into a dark alley. But something in the air around the mane of brown hair agitated and perplexed him greatly. He decided to investigate. Without much ado he pounced into the alley in pursuit of the elusive whore.

He could see that the quarry was a petite, shapely young girl. Her slender legs propelled her forwards with feline grace. He kicked up rubble and hotted the pace of the chase.

Bolt out of blue, the stoic nonchalance of indifferent masonry was silhouetted before them.

"Blind alley, thank Christ" Juan pounded along.

By this time, the girl had stopped and faced Juan with defiant bellicosity. Juan broke his speed and cautiously approached the girl, lest she should pull out some weapon. Somebody illuminated a nearly room and a beam of virgin light inundated the girls countenance. Juan stopped dead in his tracks as if struck by a bullet and collapsed prostrate.

A wild fury engulfed him as he watered the squalid dirt with hot brine from eyes. The quarry was none other than his sister Juanita.

"Why O Lord why. Why me?, why my sister?. Why us?" the words flooded his mouth. The deluge of consternation, fury and hopelessness was unabated. Tears adhered chunks of dirt on his already gummy face. He was consumed by an immediate desire to die.

Two hot drops fell and caressed his exposed neck. Juan looked up. The lachrymal repentant face of Juanita looked down. There was an expression of confused hopelessness in her eyes that wringed and bled Juan's heart to its core. He sat up.

"Why? Sister why?" Words escaped his mouth in spasmodic gasps. But they did nothing to alleviate the excruciating pain that conquered his soul.

"No money brother, absolutely no, mother is dying, what else could I do? You have forsaken us; there is nothing left with us except the house, what else could I do?"

Juanita sounded more coherent and articulate than him and her words sliced through Juan. *"If anybody is responsible it is you, you failed us, you failed your mother, You failed your sister. You lost yourself and lost us"*.

An accusing finger jabbed excoriating towards Juan. He looked at the finger and then at his sister. All last vestiges of penitence had ephermiated into thin air and a mask of naked callousness covered his face. His eyes ran dry and his throat cleared. He regained control of his speech.

"How long?" the query was prussic as it was brusque.

"Today is first. I swear by you" the defiant tone persisted.

"I'll accept that and today will be the last. Next time, I kill you straight. Is that Okay? *And I'll not fail you anymore?"*

Chapter 13

The swollen lachrymal eyes focused disconsolately at the skylight overhead. It was as though Juan expected some demi-god to incarnate at the sky-light and resurrect his mother. Juanita was sprawled in a comatose state on the same bed that once creaked under their mother's cadaverous dying self. Neighbors went about with the cursory consolation. The body was to be laid to rest in a gnarled, inelegant coffin that had been provided by a charity organization.

"The hearse has arrived" somebody shouted.

Some men bodily lifted Juan and plonked him beside the coffin of his mother on the truck where he lay dazed, totally unaware and unresponsive to the surroundings.

Some friends held him erect during the funeral and service. All the while he stared straight ahead into the vacuous flux that lay before him.

People were enacting the ritual of taking leave. Each held the hand of Juan for a few seconds before taking leave. Juan was only faintly aware of the tactile impressions conveyed by the hands. A pantomime of faintly outlined blurred faces paraded before his eyes and the heavens above were clouded with thick billows of black poisonous smoke.

His reverie was abruptly curtailed by a sonorous effeminate voice.

"I am very sorry Juan. But as you know sad and happy events have to go on. Sometimes they even occur simultaneously."

Juan woke up to see the smiling face of Vera. His paregoric, his panacea had arrived. For an instant, the heart forgot to grieve.

"Sit down Vera, sit down".

"Vera sit down, Vera, Please do sit down"

Vera kept standing and the fact that there was no seating space in the room descended upon Juan. He went red in face.

"Don't feel ashamed, I never liked formalities. But now I have a formality of fulfill. I have to invite you to my wedding. It's with Senor Gonzalez the famous jurist. Next Monday".

A thunderstorm of incredulity had broken loose over Juan's head. He stuttered and steadied and then blurted out.

"But I thought you loved me".

"What? What the hell are you speaking about? Me loving you? Are you mad? What has come over you?"

"But you must remember. We used to meet. We used to talk. Sweet talk. We even made love a couple of times – Does this not prove that you love me."

"I don't know what rubbish you are talking. If a girl meets a man once in a month or so and makes a bit of love to him, does it mean she loves him. Then whores must be in love with hundreds of people".

"But, but this is blasphemy. Christ will not forgive you".

"Learn to use your head young man. And not your heart. When you can't think, force yourself to think. If a girl loved a boy she would meet him every day".

"But the love we made. The fire we shared. You would not have surrendered yourself to me if you had not loved me. Please tell me that you love me. Please….. I implore you…. otherwise why would you have submitted yourself? Why?"

"Experience, My fine fellow. Experience. I needed Experience on how to keep men happy. And also on how to be happy myself. And that is all".

"I understand I understand". Juan held his head low. The stiletto heels were already beating retreat, as Vera retraced her steps in a huff.

"One in a million. One in a million"

He soliloquized uncontrollably – "One in a Million."

"A million, father had always said only one in a million get through the straight way. And love is no Exception".

Two hot tears streamed down his already wet cheek.

The superannuated, faded darned sheet was twisted and contorted into ungraceful unaesthetic bumps and shallows. The underside embraced the cold phlegmatic marble. On the top was sprawled a prostrate Juan. The portions of sheet near his eyes were drenched with tears. An inferno was raging within him and the profligate tears could not stifle the flames. His head was still, while his body was tossing and writhing from side to side. The fire seething within was getting out of control.

Suddenly he stood up like a spring. Then the volcano within, Erupted. Magma metamorphosed into searing molten Lava.

"God!!!!!!!!!!" the room reverberated and shook under the impact the thunderous boom.

"God, I'll take revenge. I'll get you, I tried to be all that you ever stood for. In return you destroyed my life, my world, my everything. Now Christ, I'm going to take revenge, I'm going to destroy all that you stand for, I'll destroy you, your kingdom, peace, goodness everything. Nothing I shall spare, nothing I'll teach you not to maltreat your believers. I promise, I swear by you".

Chapter 14

The derelict trunk that lay violated at his feet contained all that he needed. Pedro had always told Juan to forage in that trunk whenever there was an Emergency. And the trunk usually came up with solutions.

At his disposal lay a big magnum revolver with silencer and four magazines of twelve bullets each.

Colombia Gazette Saturday 8-12-89

Special Report: **Evening Edition**

There has been a hold up of an unusual variety in Medellin today. The robbery took place at the National Bureau of Science building near the Gymnasia crossings in Janciro section of Medellin. Today being Saturday and a half working day, there was almost no-body at the Central Administrative Building. Only two armed guards and a stock verifier were present who had kept late to complete some office-work. The guards stationed at the patio were shot clean through their heads. Then the masked and gloved intruder dragged and dumped their bodies into a culvert within the institute campus. Then the masked bandit confronted the stock verifier and led him into the main store at gun point. There the man was ordered to identify and place a variety of scientific Equipment into a trolley. The equipment included a reaction chamber, generating flasks, gas transmitters, two Weston Gas liquefying machines, a Quantatronics gas injector, Rubber Tubing's and Sealing Equipment. Also looted were two cans of 90 percent proof oxalic acid containing approximately 8 gallons of the toxic liquid and 5 packets of phosphorous pentachloride. Then the Stockist was ordered to wheel the trolley to a sports wagon that was hidden in a nearly wooded area and the loot was loaded. The masked bandit then drove off after knocking the Stockist out using the butt of his gun.

The sports wagon, a Volvo, was later found abandoned near Pensioner's Hill area. Further investigations revealed the car to be a stolen one. No finger prints or footprints are available. The marauder obviously had used flat padded shoes. A dog squad was rushed to the spot but yielded nothing. The dacoit had smothered his trail with some powerful odorous substance.

The Chief Commissioner of Medellin has voiced grave concern at the robbery and did not rule out the hand of the Cartel. At a hastily convened press conference at Press Club, he said that the oxalic acid in itself was a highly potent poison and a gallon of it in the water works could spell disaster. And to make matter worse he has confirmed that the combination of oxalic and of and phosphorous pentachloride can be used to make the deadly poison gas phosgene and that the stealing of a lot of gas collection and liquefaction equipment point to this end he added. A red alert has been sounded in Medellin and flying squads have been pat on maximum alert to meet any eventuality. A team of doctors are also ready. People have been advised not to touch any suspicious looking object and to report it to the nearest police station. The citizens are advised to carry a wet piece of cloth with them and cover their noses with it the moment they see a faint mist like gas in the air and breathe in small shallow and well spaced gaps. Investigations are continuing. The Commissioner said that he was confident of apprehending the culprits in the foreseeable future. He also recommended enhanced security at installations handling potentially dangerous chemicals.

Medellin Times-16-12-89- From Special Correspondent and the Editor's Desk

There has been another Broad Daylight robbery in the city. This robbery more than anything has thoroughly exposed the inadequacy and the deplorable state of affairs in the city security system. The robbery took place at the central High Command Station of the Homeland Security Police. A masked man, armed with a silencer equipped magnum stormed the building at around noon yesterday, when the shift change was taking place. The Commissioner of Police Mr. Rudolph O. Hara had just alighted from his high security van surrounded by security guards, when the masked marauder shot at the party using his silenced gun. The security men who could not know from where the bullets were coming and fell like flies. Four were killed on the spot and three died on the way to the hospital. Two others who were injured in the shootout are in a critical condition at and have been admitted to the Noah Foundation Nursing home.

Then the Masked Man stepped out from the gorse bush from where the executed his ambuscade and confronted the Commissioner. He look him hostage and then entered the main building. After placing the gun on the temple of the Commissioner, the Masked Man ordered all inmates to drop their arms and to assemble in the main hall. Then he commanded the men of the Riot Constabulary to step forward. They were ordered off into the store room where they were asked to place into a ruck sack twenty tear gas canisters, two launchers and two gas masks. Then he coerced the men on the pain of the death of their Commissioner to load the sack into a black Jaguar which apparently was a stolen vehicle. The Commissioner was also forced into the front seat. Then the man got into the driver's seat and chloroformed Mr. O Hara with a wad which he fished out from the glove box. The officers were dissuaded from giving a chase at the pain of the death of Mr. O. Hara.

After all this high voltage drama the man drove off. The car was later found abandoned at a perk of the ninth link road with the Commissioner still sleeping peacefully in it under the influence of the chloroform.

A special investigating team sent to the spot found no clues except the empties of .33 bore magnum. Further investigation are due and a clearer picture of this dare devil crime is expected by tomorrow morning, according to some inside sources.

Chapter 15

The tangible silence of the dimly lit room was truncated by the rhythmic monotonous glug glug of phosgene as it effervescenced from the reaction flask and meandered its way through a host of convoluted pipes to the Weston gas liquefying machine. Juan peered intently at the luminous dial inserted at the nozzle. He knew that he had the required amount when the needle transgressed the 30 mark. Slowly but inexorably the needle made steady progress towards its destination.

The church clock struck 12 pm. Almost simultaneously, as though by collusion, the meter needles also finally achieved its destination. Juan pressed a cock stop and closed the reaction chamber. Then he fitted an injector to the nozzle of the liquefier. Ten empty tear gas canisters lay at his feet. He filled then up one by one and then activated the pins and put on the catches. Now he was ready.

"Now to track that bastard, Robson Reta Muso. I'll get him soon. If only I could get the exact date of the jungle exercise."

The gyrating dusky strip tease artist removed petite bits of sequined clothing from her lascivious well oiled supple body as she whirled and twisted out in her routine. Each deft flash of hand revealed another chunk of delicious titillating flesh and provided the audience with fresh insights into her philtre.

Adolfo Balbuena did not bat an eyelid through out the show. He had seen it so many times that he had grown immune to it. Juan gawked fascinated. Adolfo was anxious to know why Juan, his bosom friend from teens, had invited him to this expensive place. Minstrel was not a place where you collect or eat your daily grub.

"So you see Addie, that is how I missed my chance. I was a bit swayed by the rubbish they belch out at the church."

"I thought you had outgrown it. But at least you have learnt now. Mark me, there is no way like the crooked way".

"Yes, yes, know. And it's funny that this crooked way is faster than the straight way".

The insipient humor in this statement struck them both and they laughed out aloud. For a moment they forgot to ogle at the porn artist.

"Now you see Addie, I want to get back on the line. And you know how difficult it is."

"Yes, the way you treated Old Muso, it's gonna be tough for you. He holds a great deal of clout you know'."

"So there is only one way. I have to do something sensational to prove myself. After all, I got disgraced from the community".

"That would attract the Family's attention. But where do I fit in?"

"I'll tell you. Something sensational I shall do and what I do, I shall do on the Family. That is where you fit in".

"I'd advise you against it. But what are you going to do?"

"I'm going to take Old Muso hostage. That is what I'll do".

"You, think you can do it?"

"Yes, I'm confident, all my plans are ready. I only need his where about".

"Nobody knows of Mr. Muso's whereabouts. That is if he has any where- about. I hear that he constantly changes his residence".

"I know, I know. I only want one piece of information, the next jungle meet. When is it going to be? Know you are under oath not to reveal it but you have to tell me".

"I don't mind doing so. The Family is also not very particular about it now-a-days. I hear that now even the police are pre-informed of it so that they can keep intruders out. Whole Medellin is under the Family now".

"Okay, then come out with it".

"You are in luck. It is this Friday".

"Thank you Addie. Thank you. I know you would help. If you need me some-day, I'll be glad to be of use".

"Anything for a friend"

And Adolfo Balbuena stood up straight like a ram rod. He was a good five inches than Juan and had an imposing personality.

The strip-teaser had come to the end of her show and had now parted her bare thighs and made an obscene gesture so that the audience could have an unhindered view of her clean shaven uvula. The people gasped. Adolfo was not interested.

He extended his right arm. Juan took it and gave it a resolute shake.

Chapter 16

The tangled undergrowth was plastered against his face, as Juan tried to wriggle into a comfortable position. Insects were mushrooming over his head in an incessant buzzing cloud. The crash suit that he wore saved him from the predicament these little monsters could deal out.

"Identifying is not going to be the problem"

Juan thought, "The limousine will be Muso's. Things have changed since I've been here last. Earlier Muso needed helicopter. Now he can strut about in his limousine. No security problems. No wonder, entire Medellin Security Forces is now theirs".

Juan's reverie was broken by unison of not too distant growls of powerful machines.

"They   are   coming"   thought Juan.   He   stiffened   and   tightened   his Crenz Avaro. The turbo lay at his feet ready to roar into life at short notice.

"I've got to merge in with the other guys. It is the only chance I've got."

Clouds of dense choking dust billowed into the foliage above, heralding the arrival of the motorcade. Sure enough, the jet black limousine was there. It was flanked on both sides by motorcycle borne guards and was followed by nearly 5 BMWs.

"Even statesmen aren't so majestic". Juan thought. He had by this time straightened the turbo. Behind the motorcade came the motorcycles.

It was a remarkable agglomeration of models and makes of all kinds and specifications. Each machine was proving its worth under some of the toughest riding conditions in the world. The motorcyclists were completely covered with an adhering canopy of billowing dust.

"It's my good luck. There has been no rain, not even a trickle in last four days. The dust makes my job Easier."

Juan roared into the group and was at once camouflaged by the common vulgar crowd around him.

"Now to keep track of Muso"; Juan thought as he spurred his machine on. He squinted hard through his visor but the cloud of dust was impregnable.

"Got to get to the front end"

Juan raced forwards. A few deft maneuvers and he was the leader. Now he could clearly see the motorcade ahead of him. It was now just a question of sticking. He religiously followed the procession out of the Jungle and into the town.

"May Fair, I should have guessed".

Juan could not help smiling inspite of himself. He arched his triplex Goodwin Tri-Star visor up to that he could get a clearer view. At a distance he saw the motorcade grind to a slow halt. A posse of beefy security men leaped out with cat like agility from the BMWs and surrounded the limousine. The gleaming black door swung wide upon. There was no mistaking the huge curved beak like nose.

"You could see it from space. So Muso, have some fun till I come back for you. First need to get to know your hole".

Juan parked his motorcycle and made leeway to a nearly bistro which advertised raw sex in bold letters. Epicurism was a way of life on Ninth Link Road and was inseparably blended to almost all aspects of life here including food. But what attracted Juan was the huge slick resplendent sheet glass façade that the bistro boasted. It's walls were as transparent as the clothes worn by its show women.

"A clear vantage view is what I get here" thought Juan as his steps altered note from the baritone thump of asphalt, to the more melodious clank of rubber soles impacting on wooden stairs of "Hill & valleys Inn". He had already identified the secretary and was now waiting for her to come out.

An impeccably attired waiter brought the Campari and soda. The sex artiste had straddled the male cast member, a big brown male, presumably a Mestizo. Juan tried his best not to get distracted. He riveted his eyes upon the entrance of May Fair and took long draughts of the bitter sweet liquor. What he liked most about Campari and Soda was that it was so much like life, bitter as well as sweet at the same time.

There was an iota of activity near the dazzling arcade of May Fair. Juan craned his neck and strained his eyes. Two young women come out. Their vinyl skirts were split in the front, a trademark of call girls. Their wallets were full and bulged outwards.

"Probably their holes are full and overflowing too?" Juan thought. The two women made beeline for "Hills and Valleys". They were courteously received at the entrance by two young women. These young women were also adorned in street walking regalia. The call-girls were offered seats and drinks by the other.

"Even in whore society there is this social ladder", Juan thought, "The younger, inexperienced and less successful respect the higher ranked ones and try to learn the finer points from the more experienced ones".

Another figure emerged from May Fair. It was the receptionist all right. Juan left the Campari unfinished and quietly slithered out. The receptionist was heading west. Juan accelerated so as to catch her just near the Volkswagen.

Delilah had another of those monotonous forgettable days behind the counter. Her cheeks were sore from the forced compulsory smile that she sported. Her voice was hoarse from shouting to obstinate recalcitrant room boys. She longed to be back home and to have a nice long reinvigorating drink. Suddenly she noticed a green Volkswagen parked near the kerb. She recognized it as her boyfriends. She double checked the number plates to make sure. She made straight for the car.

The abrupt feel of cold steel in her spine shook her rudely out of her reverie.

"Any sound, and the knife splits your spine" a husky voice growled from behind.

Delilah froze in her steps. The hair in her neck bristled up and brushed against the artificial leather of her jacket.

"Get in", the husky voice commanded. She got in. the man also got in and slammed shut the doors. She tried to identify the man from the reflection in the rear view mirror, but his face was completely covered with a muffler.

Juan pressed the knife against the receptionists' throat and growled through clenched teeth". Well Miss, All I want is some information. Do I get it? ....Or else you get it? ....Get it?"

Delilah nodded. She always maintained calm in critical and explosive situations. Her years behind the counter taught her Patience as a virtue.

"A motorcade arrived at your hotel today morning if you will remember. Now tell me where they checked into".

"You mean the hawk faced man and retinue?"

"Exactly, you got a fine head. Wow!!! Use it and remember. Where did they go?"

"That'll be easy. They had the entire third wing on second floor booked".

"Are you sure?"

"Yes, I got a photographic memory"

"Thank you Miss, You have been most co-operative. But right now you are taking a little nap in this car. And if you have lied, I come back to slit your throat without your even knowing it".

"That won't be necessary, I hope"

"Same here"

Saying this Juan took a chloroformed wad from the glove compartment. Delilah coolly submitted herself to its overwhelming smell.

In the back of the Volkswagen lay a large kitbag. It contained two silenced revolvers, two grenade launchers and 20 shells. Of these 10 shells were marked with a crude T. They contained the tear gas. The other ten contained the deadly killer fumes of phosgene. Juan picked up the two revolvers and checked their magazines. Everything was ship shape. The silencers were in position. He fired one round into the air. There was only a slight dull thud and a muted flash. So everything was okay. Juan put one revolver into his shoulder holster. The other one remained in the bag. With the bag in one hand he trudged resolutely towards May Fair.

Once near the building he scanned its surroundings to locate any extra exits. There were none. Then his eyesight drifted upwards. There it caught something gleaming against the sun. A magnificent curvilinear serpentine structure convoluted its way all up the building.

"Damn it the Fire Exit. Too late to consider it is my plane. Got to take the chance".

He entered the building through its gilded archway.

Flashing a perfunctory smile at the receptionist he sauntered along casually towards the left. A flick of a button magically transported him into the second floor. Then he hit the Fault button.

Third wing was clearly visible from the lift. The statuesque features of two beefy men were outlined against the dim corridor lightings. The aisle door was half ajar.

"Guards," thought Juan, "got to nick them off".

Standing half concealed within the shadows of the lift, he leveled and squeezed the trigger twice. The guards fell on the carpeted floor with soft, hardly audible thuds. From within the lift Juan could see that all the rooms except farthest one were open. They were jam-packed with men gulping down heady liquors.

"So Muso's up to his favorite pastime at the far end" Juan thought, "serves my purpose fine".

Bending down he unzipped the kit bag. He took out the launchers and placed them on the floor of the lift. They were aligned with the third wing aisle. He then put on the gas mask and readied the other. The launchers were then loaded with the shells marked T. Then the attack began.

Two tear gas shells whined across the still air and crashed into the walls.

Two more followed. In total ten canisters thudded into the aisle in rapid succession in salvos of two. The men inside were already gasping and spluttering. Somebody fired a gun. A slug whizzed past Juan's chin and crashed into the rosewood interior of the lift.

Quickly Juan loaded the phosgene shells and sent two of them careening into the aisle. Two more followed in a graceful arc. Then he tucked two gas grenades into his waist belt. In one hand he took the spare gas mask. In the other hand he took the loaded revolver.

The aisle had been transformed into a bedlam of anarchy. Amidst agitated and querulous expostulations, people were gasping in gulps of vaporized poison. They were all dying a slow horrible lachrymal death.

Juan stepped into the aisle and closed the door. The Juan could see through the poisonous haze that the door of farthest apartment was still closed.

"Muso do you hear me?" Juan bellowed.

"Yes, what do you want?" A voice like thunder clap boomed from within.

"I've poison gassed all your men. And you are next in line unless you open the door within thirty seconds"

"What do you mean?".

"I mean thirty seconds. Open the door and take your mask. Or else I blow the door and gas you. And don't contemplate the fire escape. My friends have it well covered".

There was a stifled groan and a few shuffling and grappling noises from within the room. All was nearly quiet in the wing as most of the men were now in a comatose state en-route to a certain death. There was an occasional wail of agony as paralysis set up in the organs. Some thrashed their arms about in a futile attempt to get up as the gas throttled them into a painful oblivion. Some had already died and their bleary eyes bulged lifeless out of their sockets. The flux was clearing by now.

"Just wait a minute" the voice was meek this time and had a distinct inflection of apprehension. Then suddenly two blasts resounded in the room and Juan could hear the thud to two bodies crashing into the wall.

"Now I am ready".

"Okay, unfasten the knob and stand back. Hands over head. Any deviation and I burst a gas grenade right under your nose and it will be bye-bye."

The handle turned and there was the sound of retracing feet. Juan burst in and slammed the door behind. Muso stood before him hands raised over head, completely nude. He stiffened as Juan pointed the silenced gun at him. On the floor lay the corpses of two young women. Both were naked except for open shirts. The pubic region of one of them was wet. Scarlet blood oozed out from holes neatly punctured in between their eyes. Their nipples were erect. They were probably in that state when rigor mortis had set in.

"Okay Muso, We are going for a Ride."

"Should I not clothe myself first."

"Of Course, You Must. Please help yourself".

"The Mask, Please give it to me".

"Nope. first you clothe. Any tricks and I blow the Grenade in my Belt before I die. Now get moving. Or you too get wasted like the girls."

"Now wear this' Juan handed over the mask to Muso. He strapped it on "Moving?" said Juan and shoved Muso with the muzzle of his gun. He hurriedly trotted towards the door.

Once they were out of the aisle, Juan ordered a visibly trepidated Muso to a halt. He then ordered him brusquely out of his mask. He replaced both the masks and grenades in the kitbag. He took out a tweed blazer and draped his hand with it so as to conceal the gun.

"Okay, now easy steps. Any false move and your spine is split".

Muso shuddered and shuffled on, trying to retain as much equanimity as he could. There was a cold iniquity and tautness in Juan's impassive tone that sent a shiver down his spine.

The lift was not there in place. The display showed it to be en-route to somewhere nearing the penthouse.

"We take the stairs", the succinct orders of Juan were nearly dementing to Muso. Never in his life had he had to climb stairs. "At least it is going down", he consoled himself.

Soon the two were trotting down the balustraded red carpeted stairs.

"Now, move softly and casually, or else it's your spine before you even know it."

The sun was beating down stoically inspite of the incept of ameliorated autumn.

Chapter 17

"Towards the greed sedan". Juan barked. Soon they were near the gleaming profligate being of the sedan.

"Now you hitch out the Trunk" Juan ordered.

Muso nodded in sullen condescence.

Once the kit bag was loaded Juan ordered Muso to the front.

"Open the door and get in. We drive straight to your office. And don't forget to put down this sleeping beauty at Amours Park".

———◆———

"Muso, you may assume your seat. May I have the pleasure of calling you Mr. Robson". Juan's voice had a courthouse intonation now.

A visibly dazed and shaken Robson staggered and planked into his velvet veloured revolving chair.

"Now you must be wondering why I took all this trouble just to bring you to your office?"

"Yes, yes why the hell....." inspite of the cordial inflexion in Juan's tone, the truculent stance of the silenced gun persisted unabated. Robson bit his lips as he tried to stifle the abusive verbal broadside ones that played on his tongue.

"Let us be short, brief and to the point. It saves time and energy. ***The contract Mr. Robson Reta Muso,…. the contract. …I want back my contract***". Juan's rhetoric was brusque.

"Oh, that's all" Robson asked in an honestly invidious voice, his face reflecting his utter flabbergastedness.

"Yes, that is all. Fish out the contract I'll sign it here and now. I know the Family respects its contracts."

"That was all,….. only that", the element of incredulity continued in Robson's voice, "Why all this mess? This was absolutely uncalled for. You could have just strolled in and asked for it. After all you are Pedro's brother."

"Don't pretend Muso, You know it would not have been that easy. Now men are more and jobs are less.

More people go empty bellied in Shanty-town because far more officials are corrupt nowadays. So far far less work and a rush of men to do it. I knew I had to prove myself. And I did. I hope. Haven't I? Most respected Mr. Robson Reta Muso?"

"Yes, Yes, yes you have. In fact in future I'm going to recommend the most vital missions to you. You are the man we were looking for. Singlehandedly you wiped out the entire constabulary of Muso and had him groveling as your hostage. You are indeed the finest in the trade. I am constantly not going to risk losing you a second time. Just a moment".

Muso opened a mahogany cabinet in his desk and fished out an ebony colored flared dossier.

"I'm putting a few crosses. Sign wherever you see one. Then take this card. With you give it to the cashier as you go out. He will give you fifty thousand Pesos. Summons will be sent to you whenever required. Your monthly allowance shall be sent by cheque. And of course there is bonus after every successful mission depending upon the importance of the mission. And don't you ever feel anxious with regard to Juanita. From this very moment she is the Family responsibility, not yours. By the way you are still holed up in Pensioner's Hill I suppose?"

"Good, your cheques will arrive there. Get a phone installed for summons".

"Now you may go"

"Thank you, Sir".

Chapter 18

There were no histrionics, no wishy-washying, and no lachrymal excesses. Juan had just said a plain naked goodbye to his sister as she stood like a rock watching him ascend the gnarled steps of the rugged pick up van. The summons had come and there was no looking back.

The mass of the truck creaked and jostled with itself as it groaned recalcitrantly into a rather peevish start. It was as though on old man was forced to creak open his arthritis ravaged joints on a damp chilly day to take a morning walk. The truck gave a sharp lurch as though expressing its indignance and was soon on its way.

"This Family. It's funny the way they retain trucks. They and their superstitions". Juan thought as he browsed over the morning paper. The capricious suspension of the dilapidated truck was taking heavy toll on all.

"All the stuff of this lucky truck, my left foot. Ant it's the poor Juan's who are at the receiving end. Our bad luck that this shaker had to be the lucky truck. I wish somebody would burn it to cinders".

Juan's patience was running thin. He flung the paper out in disgust. In the truck more vital jobs like preventing a joint dislocation had to be attended to.

"Take one ride to have a rib dislocated and then another to jarr it back into place". Juan smiled to himself.

But this wreck of a truck was a priceless jewel for the superstitious top brass of the cartel. For the past ten years, successful missions were always initiated by this lucky truck. To summon the henchman in this truck was tantamount to hiring lady-luck along with the killer free of cost. Or so it had happened in the past one decade. And the mentors had immense faith on this misery on wheels.

The man who greeted Juan was impeccably attired and smooth talking. He ushered him into a large spacious and amply furnished hall.

"Have your seat please". It was the smooth talking man. His accent was infallible and manner extremely blandishing.

A liveried attendant brought in a bottle of champagne and two glasses. The agent poured out two glasses.

"My esteemed pleasure, My dear fine young man to offer you a drink".

Juan accepted the champagne without any rituals or ceremony.

He drained his glass without waiting for his host to touch his own.

The agent was unruffled by Juan's behavior.

"Now the work, if you please my dear fine young gentleman." The voice was as courteous as eternity.

"Get on with it". This voice was as unceremonious as ever.

"Maybe the knowledge has filtered to your ears that our most respected and benevolent benefactor, the Godfather has been implicated."

"Yes, it did. In fact the papers were full of it. I hear the judgment is to be on twenty first".

"What is today?"

"The first of course. What about it?"

"That means you get exactly twenty days".

"Twenty days what do you mean? Come out with all of it. I don't like puzzles."

"Okay; my dear fine young fellow. I will act exactly as you wish. To put it as scantly and sweetly as possible, you are to bid a nice 'definitive adios' to Mr. Hugo Almeido the sitting Grand Judge of Medellin High Court".

"How is that going to help?'

"He is the one to deliver the judgment on the twenty first. And he is indeed a very foolish man".

"Have you tried paying him off?"

"We in the Family are no butchers. We have great regard for the purpose and sanctity of human life. We try all possible means before taking the extreme decision. But as I said before this Hugo, he is a very foolish man,… very foolish."

"And as I said before. How's this murder going to help?"

"The second judge Silvio Suarez is our man. He is the man slated to accede Mr. Hugo. Once Hugo is out, Silvio becomes the Grand Judge. Now you understand how?"

"Yes I do".

"My secretary sitting in the adjacent room will supply you with the details of the job-. And need I repeat it, failure with not be accepted or tolerated".

Chapter 19

"If there is a man of character in this wretched God forsaken country its Senor Hugo".

Heads bobbed up and down in silent agreement. The coffee mugs were steaming and beer jugs frothing.

"Will he last?"

"He has lasted so long"

"But how far"

"With God's Grace maybe much much Far"

You forget even God's grace depends upon the cartel here"

"I heard he is going to try Godfather and he will be tough with him"

"If he does so it'll create history."

"When is the judgment?"

"About twenty days from now"

"Hope that he lasts for at least those twenty days".

"He'll be bumped off"

"Now you, its bastards like you who demoralize the public and let them be herded by the Mafioso like sheep"

"I just like speaking the truth. And mind you, don't raise your voice so high lest you meet the same fate as this poor judge is gonna get"

"You swine, People like you are destroying this country"

"Men men, there'll be no-quarrelling in this bar. Any body who squabbles clears off. I hope that is clear".

——◆——

"Catch a man by his hair, throat or by his testicles. Grab his vulnerable point"

Father's words dawned upon Juan as he brooded over a Marlboro. The information was all there in the dossiers supplied by Robson's agent.

Mr. Hugo Almeido, thirty five, 5'10", dark, handsome non smoker teetotaler, Methodist, wife, one teenaged laughter, one seven year old son. House virtually impregnable, guarded by 8 special protection force commandos, 16 Doberman pinschers. Two barbed wire fences. An electrified barrier and sophisticated alarm devices and closed circuit cameras.

Moves about in a bullet proof car. All visitors to pass through metal detectors, Court sessions well guarded.

Personal qualities:- Introvert, non-socialite, dedicated family man.

Wife. -Rarely seen in public, reserved woman.

Daughter: Abroad at some unknown destination.

Son: Tutored at home by Mr. Perez Roldan.

"A good morning to you, my pretty Senorita, can I meet Senor Robson".

"Good day to you, But right now Senor Robson is engaged, can you wait till some other date".

"No, the nature of my work is urgent"

"Could you tell me what you want?"

"All I want is some information. I need to know more of this Perez Roldan, the man who tutors Hugo's son".

"In future sir, you'd better forward such requests directly to me. Senor Robson does not like to be disturbed for such minor things. The dossier, shall reach you by tomorrow".

"As you wish"

"Perez Roldan, widower, 52, B.A, 12, Quentin Forde Avenue, One Sister, brother in law 5 children, address-24. Queens road, Educated, smooth talking. No criminal record, cocaine addict, moderate drinker, limited night life, non-smoker".

Teacher at Mount Carmel, non-socialite. Introvert, secretive. Strongly attached to his sister.

⊷⊗⊶

"Recognize the lady in this photo?".

"Why yes! Oh No! Oh god! You got my sister but why? Please don't harm her. This the only one left in this world who loves me. Please don't harm her."

"We won't. At least not for the time being".

"But why? Why should you imprison us both?. I swear both of us have led clean lives thro-out".

"Your life is not gonna be clean any more. Your sister is going to take care of it. Now tell us about your good master Senor Hugo Almeido".

"Well, I tutor his son at home and that is all I know about him".

"We'd like you to kill him".

"Kill him?"

"You must be mad. I can never do a thing like this to Senor Hugo, I've always adored him. His never treated me slightly. I can never dream of any such thing. No".

"I believe you adore your sis even more than Senor Hugo or have I got it wrong?"

"What do you mean?"

"One of them have to go. I have got it right this time. You understand brother".

"You can't do this to me".

"We can do more, and more and yet even more. To you and your damn what???.. Yes, Sister, May be even in your presence. I don't think you'd wish me to elaborate".

"Will you set her free if I do your dirty work?"

"Yes I promise"

"How am I to believe you".

Juan's face contorted into a most vicious scowl. His lips quivered with anger as he bellowed-"*Your damn politicians. The politicians for whom you vote for, they are the liars. They promise you heaven and what you get it worse than hell. You can believe them but not me. You can vote for them but mot bank on my word. You cheer for them but look at me with hatred in your eyes. That is what makes you what you are. A poor miserable wretch. What have you got from trusting those fucking politicians??...... Anything?... No!,.... Nothing. .... But you can't trust me*".

"I trust you sir". A strange calmness had possessed the voice of Perez.

"Are we making progress?"

"I need some time, sir"

"There is no time, Sir, you have to tell me your decision now and only now?"

"Yes Sir"

"What, yes Sir? Tell me what?"

"I mean Yes, Sir"

"Good, Remo, give this man a good breakfast. We talk after breakfast."

———— ❦ ————

"Okay, Senor Perez. What is a day like for you at the Hugo household?"

"Pretty simple Sir. I go there at 5.0" clock. I get frisked by guards and get shoved around with a metal detector. Then I go inside and give little Monzon lessons till seven. Then Monzon changes into his beautiful red bathing trunk and we……"

"Just a moment. Why only red bathing trunk?"

"Because Sir, Little master is obsessed with red. He wears red, plays red, eats red and sleeps on red".

"Hmm. that is interesting. Please proceed".

"By this time Senor Almeido arrives and little master jumps into his lap and gives him a three minute kiss".

"Wait a minute. Does this take place every day?"

"Yes sir, it's become almost a ritual".

"Very good. And does little Monzon always wear his bathing trunks when he smooches over his father."

"Almost always sir. That is about the time Senor Almeido comes home from his morning stroll. And punctuality is one of his qualities".

"I know that. Now there is one little thing I'd like to ask you. How does little Monzon change this clothes".

"Oh Sir, he is a very shy boy. Would never let me see his unmentionables. He gets into an attached closet and throws out his clothes one by one. Then he calls for his trunk which I threw in. Then he gets out ready for the swim".

"Excellent, beautiful. Thank you Senor Roldan, thank you very much. You may go now. You shall receive instructions and equipment in the afternoon. In the meanwhile be our honored guest".

Chapter 20

"Well Senor, I hope you have rested well and are ready for our little work".

"As you say, Sir"

Juan was sitting on a Victorian style swivel chair. A fake Chippendale adorned the left side of the chair. A richly inlaid, ivory manacled Indian Lamp stand flanked his right. On the fake Chippendale, lay a contemporary Styrofoam kit bag.

Perez squinted from behind his bifocals trying to make out the contents of the bag.

Two graceful curvaceous seminude feminine characters supported the lamp stand on their shapely bare breasts. It was truly a magnificent example of-"Finesse and craftsmanship".

Perez was visibly uncomfortable in his straight backed satin velour chair. A relaxed seat on this vertical back type seat requires a perfect posture and a fine alignment of the thoracic vertebra.

He squinted from behind his bifocals trying to make out the content of the kit bag from its bulges.

"Care for a puff"

"Thank you, sir"

"Here is the light"

"Now that you are relaxed and rested, Senor Roldan, your briefing begins now".

A nerve throbbed in Perez's temple and cold sweat tricked down his nose and eyebrows misting his bifocals. The cigarette smoldered nonchalantly in his immobilized fingers.

Juan undid the zipper of the kit bag and brought out a packet. He opened it and held out the contents in the light for Perez to see.

"What do you see my dear man?"

"Bathing trunks sir?"

"What else do you see? I mean what else can you say of this?"

"Children's trunks Sir……….. And yes, the color Sir, its red. The same as that little master loves."

"Exactly, My dear brother, Brilliant. A children's bathing trunk in red. The very color Monzon likes. Nice one isn't it. But one small difference. This one is lined on the inside with high intensity plastic explosive instead of latex".

Perez gulped for air like a baited carp. All he could say was a shriveled muffled "Yes, Sir".

Juan thrust his strong arms into the packet again and this time brought out a waist belt.

"I have noticed that you wear belts because you are too thin for the cheap readymade clothes you use".

"Yes, Sir"

Juan held the belt up in the light to emphasize it.

"This belt you see is made of cheap artificial leather. But the buckle made of steel and as you can see appears a bit oversize".

Juan tipped the belt slightly so that Perez could see the silhouette distinctly.

"You see this projection" Juan pointed to a tiny obtrusion to one side of the buckle which was now accentuated by its shadow, "This is the triggering device. A detonator inside the trunks gets activated by this. Press this and Ka- Boom!!!! Understood? To prevent accidental ignition there is a safety catch just below the button. Here it is".

Indeed there was a slight sliding strip impaled into a groove.

"You push the strip into the button like this," Juan pressed the strip nimbly with his thumb, "and it goes click behind the button. Now an accidental push can't press it. You are to keep it this way till you get into the residence. Right?"

"Yes, Sir"

"You keep it as it is till you are ready. Then you press the end of the strip and out it comes. Okay?"

"But how do I take the whole thing into that place. The mansion is a real fortress Sir, guards, metal detectors, dogs, barbed wire and what not. I've been working there for so many years now. It's impenetrable. There are no chinks in its armor. At least not as far as I know".

"Exactly, not as far as you know. But there is one small chink in the armor of Senor Hugo Almeida and that Senor Roldan, is you".

"Me? What me? How?. I don't understand sir".

"You will, as I have noticed you got a very slender waist and I suppose you will have no difficulty in slipping on a child's trunks. True?"

"Yes sir, But…………"

"No ifs and buts entertained. You'll be wearing the trunks under your pants and the belt over it. The detonator has been placed in the trunks to coincide exactly with the remote trigger. And you'll wear them both such that the mid seam of the trunk and your buckle are exactly over your manhood, right on the median line of your balls. Understood? Wait a minute. In this way the buzz of the detonator will be confused with the buzz of your belt buckle. And they are both made of same metal. So you get right through the metal detector. Yes, now what were you saying?".

"Sir, excuse me sir, but I could get blown to bits if there is any malfunction."

"Yes true. Very true, you do stand a fifteen percent chance of getting blown into bits yourself. By this way you get a seventy-five percent survival chance. The other alternative is a zero percent survival chance for you and an equally bright survival chance for your dear sister. Now the choice is yours."

The silence that ensued was tangible and Roldan pondered over the turn of events. Finally a grim grin sliced his face.

"Okay Sir. But how do I get the explosive to Senor Hugo".

"Good question, you are picking up the scent. Little Monzon is going to do us this little favor."

"What do you mean? What exactly do you mean".

"When Monzon steps into the closet you open your pants. Then you swap his trunks for yours. Then when Monzon embraces his father, you press our little button. Pretty simple isn't it?"

"Simple? Is it? You goddamn bastards. Heaven will never forgive you for this? What harm did that angel do to you beasts? Why do you have to kill him? Beasts? Why do you have to kill him? Tell me why? Tell me?" Perez had never hollered like this before in his life.

"Calm down Senor. Roldan, or else we may have to do the same to you. As you know some sacrifices have to be made for attainment of higher goals. Being a school master you know that only too well. Besides your sweetie-cums sissy. Whom would you like to sacrifice? Little Monzon or your sweet sibling?"

"You, you are butchers. No, you are even worse than that. You are murderers. You are Satan. All of you".

"I'm sorry, Senor. But it is our trade you see, circumstances do affect men. Once I was also like you, God-fearing, Satan hating and so on. But I can't help it now. Now you'd better calm down. Or the consequences shall be, well..........you understood I believe".

Perez was shaking with uncontrollable rage. He bit his lip in a savage attempt to leash the simmering volcano of hatred and indignation within and prevent it from erupting. As he bit hard, hot blood drained down his chin and dropped into his lap with a splat. The splat and the sight of blood steadied him a bit. He looked at the blotch of blood on the linen of his shirt and suddenly he could see his sister in it completely engulfed by that one little blotch of blood. He closed his eyes and wept, trying to shirk away from the blood curdling apparition. He wept for his sister. He wept for himself. He wept for mercy. He wept for deliverance. He wept.

"I hope that feels better now that you have wept". Juan's ice cold tone seared into Perez's ear and tore into his thought.

With one massive herculean effort he steadied himself. He had decided. He will commit the crime. After all what had god given him in return for his years of uncomplaining subservience?

"Now let me serve Satan for a while. I presume the days God ruled earth are over. Perhaps Satan and God had a big fight over earth at some time. And probably God was vanquished. It is Satan who rules earth now. We are his subjects. Anyone who dares defy him must suffer. Like me. Like my sister. We defied him throughout our lives so far. And we are paying the price now. And Satan's loyal subjects. They rule the Earth. Just look at my captor. Look at his opulence, his splendor. So many more like him there are out there. Nobody can count. Cannot forgive God for landing me in this inspite of my years of devotion. Patience has a limit, let me try appeasing Satan. Perhaps he will forgive me after all and shower upon me what he bestows on the other faithful."

"Yes Sir, I'll do it"

"Good, make sure you are within five meters of Hugo when Monzon embraces him. Then you press the button. The triggering device has a range of seven meters. And the explosive has a kill blast radius of three meters. So five meters would be safe either way. Our men will give you the final briefing. Now we arise. We expect tonight to be Senor Hugo's last. I hope you won't fail the trust we imposed on you".

"Yes, Sir, I'll do my best".

"Good! Now good luck and take care you have my best wishes".

"Thank you Sir"

"But one thing. How do I get out, Sir after the business?"

"Yes, I forgot, Damn. I always keep forgetting things these days. Immediately after the blast you make for the rear door. My marksmen there will eliminate all guards & dogs and blast the barricades. After all guards don't wear flak jackets or move around in bulletproof glass. That part will be easy. Okay!"

"Yes, Sir"

"And after, I'm free"

"Oh, sure"

"Are you sure this rat is gonna die too?"

"Almost. The explosive has a kill range of seven meters. If he keeps within the five meters I prescribed, he'll be free as he wished. He'll be free of this material world within a fraction of a second. If he escapes, well that is another head ache altogether".

"Got to see a doc. Well in your case what I prescribe is this."

Chapter 21

Senor Hugo Almeido and his darling son Monzon ran towards each other from opposite ends of the hall.

"Oh, my little cherub, my heart, my soul come into my arms".

Filial affection wafted through the air and the aroma of parental pride hung heavy in the air. Monzon's doting mother, her eyes brimming with star dust and moonlight, feasted her eyes on the approach of the two souls and one body. She stood near the mantelpiece where the twain met every day.

Quivering fumbling steps burdened Perez to a place within five meters of the mantelpiece. His tongue went dry and a thousand tiny bubbles seem to rise within his guts and crash against his heart. The seemingly choreographed ritual of father son union seemed to his eyes to be a slow motion replay of the original. Too slow, painfully slow. A grim smile adorned his gnarled cheeks as he took the only four confident decisive steps he had taken in the whole evening. The rest were all an amalgamation of hobbling, wobbling, quivering steps a stealthy slinking gait. There was a satisfied look in his eyes. A furrow or two smoothed themselves out into extinction from his barnacled forehead. It was as if a great load had been taken off his shoulders. As if he had found a way out.

Yes, very true. Indeed for those few moments Senor Perez Roldan had the peace of mind that had evaded him since the morning. He had found a way yes, a way, a way out a way out from all that stood against him, his duty, his conscience. He had found a way to save his sister, as well as his honor. He had found a way of reprieve, of relief to his sister's material sufferings and his emotional. Yes, true, indeed where there is a will, there is a way.

Those, four steps brought him to within three meters of the mantelpiece.

Monzon buried his head into his father's lap. Hugo entwined his arms around his half naked son. Mrs. Almeido glided towards them in a wave of doting admiration.

Then Perez pressed the button.

Daily Mail
Date; 14/12/79 Day: Sunday

In what appears to be a suicide attack, Senor Hugo Almeido, Grand Judge, Medellin High Court, was assassinated at about 7.0" clock yesterday. Senor Almeido, son Monzon, his wife and Senor Perez Roldan, his seven year old son's tutor, are among the deceased. The explosive device that caused the catastrophe is widely believed to have been smuggled in by the tutor Perez Roldan. A security guard posted at the Almeida residence has confided on conditions of anonymity that Senor Perez's clothes did respond in the affirmative to the metal detector test. But the security cordon had let him through as the source of the signal seemed to be a metallic buckle that Senor Perez wore on his belt.

Senior investigating officer Jorga Vincent is of the view that the belt must have been lined inside with plastic explosives and the buckle was a disguised detonator. Perez's sister Tanya is missing and a nationwide alert is on for her. Her photograph and details are given below and anybody having any information about her is requested to contact the police. The Roldan's residence at, 12 Quentin Forde, has been sealed and all their property has been attached.

The word that is about here is that the cartel is involved in this gruesome assassination. Senor Almeido was to deliver an important judgment on a top Kingpin of the Cartel, who has been charged with a second degree murder and drug running, in about a week. Now it seems the judgment shall be deferred for some other day. It is widely believed that in the interval the cartel will gather enough evidence to free their man.

According to a late report received just now Senor Silvio Suarez has been appointed as the Grand Judge at the High Court of Medellin with effect from tomorrow. He is expected to take charge in a week time.

"What about her?"

"It has been taken care of."

"What do you mean?"

"Just what I said. But don't worry. The whole thing was painless. She was sleeping peacefully, when I slit her neck. She didn't feel a thing."

"I tell you this is hideous. This is just hideous. You can't do this. I had given the word to the dead man."

"Keep your head Juan. Here it is not your or mine word that counts. The word of the Family is final. Besides who knows better than you that there is no place in this world for honest hardworking idiots like her. She'll be better off in heaven. Now have a cigar and cut it out. Lives like hers aren't worth a quarter."

"Then you tell me what is worth one."

Vicario was taken aback by Juan's question. He stared into heavens for a second as if expecting the answer to come from the almighty himself. Then a confused look came over his hungry features.

"Perhaps the cigar you are puffing at" he suggested.

Even Juan had to strain a smile through his clenched teeth into the cloud of smoke in his front. One by one his stiffened features loosened. Vicario stared disinterested into the vacancy in his front.

Juan's jaw was the last to unwind.

"You don't have a sister do you?"

"Of course not", Vicario pondered over the relevance of the question. "How did you know?"

"Just intuition"

"Do you have one"

"Now, let us leave the matter. How about a beer"

"Fine idea"

Chapter 22

Browsing over the strong morning coffee, Juan rummaged with scant regard for detail, through the pages of the paper. All of a sudden two soft palms entombed his eyes in a shroud of darkness. As he blinked into the darkness ahead, a summer voice rang euphoniously into his ears "Guess who?"

"A she-ape. I presume".

Juanita gave Juan's head such a violent shake that he almost let go the mug of coffee safely clasped in his hand.

She had indeed blossomed ravishingly. As she curled herself into the sofa Juan could not help but notice the almost coquettishly feline grace she had acquired over the years.

Almost at the same instant, he was angry with himself. It was almost as if an inner hand had delivered a sharp slap across his cheek. Juan grimaced with pain.

"You don't think of such things about your sister understand,"

A voice inside him reprimanded.

He always found it funny that a murderer like him should suffer from these bouts of conscience. He always felt that it was an alter-ego to the calloused murderer that he was. He always felt a different person when not at work.

There was this inner eye, second being, an inner voice and intellect that used to always sum up, observe, evaluate and judge his actions. No matter how insignificant an issue might be, this meddlesome inner self just would not desist from, or rather resist from poking its nose. It would pass the judgment; whether the contemplated action was right or wrong and accordingly order Juan. It was really funny how this voice ruled the brighter side of his life. The darker side was a like a bad dream, a nightmare to be lived through and be forgotten.

"Really Funny"

"What is so funny?"

"Oh, nothing really".

"What is this Brother, Most of the times I see you go off into a trance and then you start mumbling something? You almost don't live in this world. Why do you brood so much?"

"Now leave it. My nature, so I brood. You are of the bubbly kind. So you fritter away your energy without any reason. And by the way, I notice you are bubblier than usual today. What's the matter?"

An abashed look came over her face. She first surveyed her impeccable Gucci's and then her neatly manicured nails. Then she looked up apologetically.

"I'm getting married".

"What?"

This time the mug of coffee got the better of Juan, and its glee was evident as it splashed down Juan's neatly pressed trousers.

"Oh, Damn, the fucking......"

But, the marriage? What are you saying? When? Whom? I don't understand."

"I'm sorry I didn't tell you, it's the Commissioner. Adolfo, Adolfo Jara".

"Merciful Heavens, bless me. What are you saying? That Jara, the Commissioner. Of all the persons in the world you had to pick him. Don't you know his connections with the Mafioso? Don't you read the paper?"

"But you are also in it. And I don't disown you or blame you for it".

"That's because you can't. I tried to eat some honest bread. And failed. I had no choice. You think this bastard from those fucking upper class had no choice".

"Nobody has no-choice in this god-forsaken land. There are only two options. Be with them, or........ be with god. My fiancé is no exception to the jungle law that rules this asylum".

"I guess you are right"

"Besides he is so handsome and is so nice to me. He is as beautiful as was Pedro."

Juan's face clouded as furrows streaked across his forehead.

"I'm sorry brother"

"It's okay"

"I know how fond you are of him even now"

"Now leave that. When is it gonna-be"

"The next Thursday. Oh! I'm so so happy I' so happy that I can't even describe it."

"You are happy, that's enough for me. Congratulations. No questions asked".

"Just one more thing to make me happy".

"Anything I'll do for you, do see a smile on your face bloom o-o-oh"

"This is serious".

"Okay, fire away"

Juan had never felt this light and bouncy in eons. He knew not why. But his inner self seemed to be obsessed with this emotional trampoline and merrily it bounced away.

"I know you people kill as your boss says and are very dedicated. You would kill your father if they said so".

Juanita had decided to be as blunt as was possible.

"Awww… ho, killing, killing, killing, killing subject on my head here also, can't you change the topic". The trampoline had slackened and his inner self failed to gather momentum for one more bounce.

"Just can't. It's something I wanted to talk to you long back. Promise me that you won't kill Adolfo on order from anyone whomsoever."

"Oh, that's all. I wouldn't dream of such thing rest assured, Wish granted".

"Oh, brother you are such a dearie". Juanita voice sang with joy as she enveloped her nice dear brother in a huge hug and then ran out.

Trampoline tightened yet again. Juan was happy. Real happy. So so happy that he wished he had a little sadness to dilute his happiness. He was not used to happiness for so so long. It was almost like a teetotaler getting drunk on a Bloody Mary.

At least for once, at least for once he had proved his father wrong. Juanita was among the one in a million who found true love. She was among the one in millions who are going to lead a life where comfort is not antagonistic to self esteem, where pleasure is not a bed fellow of riches, where kindness is not adulterated with pretence, where love is not tainted with treachery, where........... where............ He had wished, he had cringed, he had beseeched before the almighty, for once, ...just for once, he wanted to disprove his father. They, the children of god, children of dust, children of sweat blood and tears could also be among the one in a million. Oh how happiness flowed. Ride on merry angel, let God be the wind beneath your wings.........

"Juanita is among the one in a million" He shouted.

Chapter 23

There was blood. There was sweat, there were tears. The crimson patch on the disheveled crumpled virgin white sheets bore testimony that a virgin had been deflowered today. Sweat poured from the two bodies that thrashed and swayed in a crescendo celebrating un-adulterated passion. Tears of Joy welled in the eyes of Juanita.

Juanita let out a contented sigh.

Adolfo's thought train continued, "I hate to do it but she is the only one so mad enough in love with me so as to believe everything that I say. I don't like doing this to his but I needed a façade. At least a married man would be less suspect. It was lucky I made through this. I don't know how many more times I shall be able to repeat this pretence".

"How was I?" Juanita's voice was hoarse and had a tinge of expectancy around it.

Adolfo stiffened. He knew exactly what she had in mind. A second course. And he certainly would not be able to participate in the feast. He had to take evasive action fast.

"Oh my sweetie-cums. You were terrific. One Round with you and all my juice is yours. I don't know what is there in you that milked me real dry in just one go. Absolutely exhilarating"

"You, mean no more play today?"

Juanita's voice was both accusing and dejected.

"I think perhaps no. The wedding hassles really took everything out of me".

"It's okay. No need to be apologetic. After all we got our whole life before us. What's more important is that I love you and you love me. Don't you Darling?"

"Of course I do – That's no question to ask".

"I was just kidding. Let's go to sleep"

Juanita reached out and turned the lights off.

Sleep was not far behind. With sleep come torrid dreams of steamy passion.

Adolfo dreamt too. He dreamt of Black Pearl, Pablo's smooth ass, Pablo's thick lips, his sexy stubble.

"Hey Juan, I want to have a word with you"

"Of course Almo. What's it?"

"Heard your sister got married"

"Yeah it is true. The happy day was day before yesterday".

"And is it true that your sister married the commissar Adolfo?"

"Yes perfectly true".

"Are you sure the Family is going like this?"

"No problem. Adolfo is their man, he is ours".

"Oh, that's a big relief."

"But tell you one thing. I've seen Adolfo in and out of Black Pearl many a time."

"What Black Pearl? The gay hangout"

"Yeah, the gay palace"

"Are, you sure?"

"Yup"

"Must have been after some creeps or wierdos. Adolfo is very strict on them you know".

"But he was never in uniform".

"Is it?"

Juan's brain was slightly jolted as he grappled with certain unholy thoughts that had intruded upon his serene mind. But he was not going throw away his newly infused faith in God that easily.

"Ah you Bloody Bloody fool. Don't you know policeman mostly take up these assignments in plain clothes."

"That is true. But so many times..........."

"Because there are so many creeps and now shut up you are spoiling my mood and my mind".

Chapter 24

"You are late again"

"Sorry Juanita Darling. This work. It's just killing me."

"Work, what work? I never saw you work so much before. Remember during our courtship we used to have our dates right in your office. Never saw any work then".

"Things have changed now dear."

"How come? Have you turned against the Family? Or is there a new Family against the old."

"It's not like that. You won't understand. What can I say?"

Adolfo paused for a minute and thought of something.

"Anyway these things are pretty shut up kind. I cannot say anything you know. So please don't ask me further".

"Okay Senor Commissar. If you insist so. Okay, but look I'm a woman. A young woman. And I love you. I love life. I can't go on for ever like a machine. Even machines need servicing."

"I understand. But please try to understand me. I just can't help it". Suddenly Juanita stood up. A look of beastlike ferocity and wistful intensity came into her eyes. She moistened her dry lips with the soothing caress of her quivering tongue. With one swift motion she untied the knot of her gown. And swiftly she fell upon the sofa and spread her legs wide apart so that her essentials stared right into Adolf's face. "Just look at her" Juanita pointed point blank at her spot, "Just look at her. See if this helps you". Her voice was hoarse but confident. Adolfo was aghast. But the look of amazement on his face swiftly dissolved into reeking disgust.

"Just cover it up? Please cover it up. Such things are expected only from a streetwalker. Not from you, the respectable wife of a respectable commissar. Cover it".

"Cover it, my foot", Juanita was screaming.

"Such things are expected only of street walkers. That's what you said isn't it? Don't be surprised if I walk the streets. Not for money thanks to you, but for sex, also thanks to you. Then we shall see how respectable you are."

"I hate you Adolfo. I hate you. Get out of my sight". Juanita was screaming herself hoarse. But the confidence that rang in her voice was missing now.

She could understand the look of amazement, but that of reeking, disgust? That was incomprehensible. She always thought men loved such sights. Especially young men. They would give anything for it. She also believed that women could always stir up a man, a young one at least, whenever she wanted. Or was she wrong? Was it a myth? She wondered. The confidence was missing.

Adolfo slammed the door behind him.

Chapter 25

"Hi Dear, meet my friend Pablo. This is my wife, my life, Juanita".

"Liar" was Juanita's rapprochement, though it was intended to sound, "Hi Senor Pablo, Nice to meet you".

"Pablo is my friend, my assistant, my right hand-man".

Adolfo was virtually gushing over Pablo.

"There is no man with as much grey matter in Colombia as Pablo. He's a real stud, a real smash. Finest policeman I've ever seen, great man........."

"That's enough praise", Juanita icy tone sliced sharply across Adolfo's tribute to Pablo.

"I understand that you are both great friends, Senor Pablo. Please be seated. Care for a drink?"

It was Adolfo who replied. "Seated will be. But in my room. Now listen Juanita, this is important. We've got a top mission on-our hands. This requires a lot of planning. So me and Pablo are going to be in my room, locked up for at least two hours. We don't want anybody disturbing us. Not even you darling. I hope you understand. Tell the servants too, please".

All Juanita could offer was a mumbled okay and a pair of rose bud lips for cursory kiss.

She did not mind, but somehow she was not rest assured.

She could not understand show an indolent officer and a compulsive bribe taker like Adolfo suddenly got interested in important missions. She also did not like Pablo. She didn't like the way he shuffled uneasily while he walked, his unsure gait, his squirming and shifting, his uneasy glance, and inability to look into one's eye when talked to. And she certainly hated the half mischievous half taunting crooked smile that he gave her. She really hated him.

Yes, she was not convinced, certainly not. She was confident of Adolfo but this Pablo. He inspired anything but confidence. Was he blackmailing her husband? Was he threatening him? Was he conspiring with him?

"Listen Adolfo, Mister Commissar, shucks to you and your duty. I certainly don't know what is this mission that keeps you and Pablo huddled in your room well past midnight and you away from me all nights. It has been ten days since you slept with me. Not that it really helped. But still the touch of yours warm body was some balm to my disappointment. My question is how long more? Tell me how long more I've to keep up with this".

Adolfo gulped as he searched for the right words and the right inflexion of tone to offer. Finally in a heavy voice, overdosed with repentance, "It'll soon be over, my darling, It'll soon be over. And I will make up on all the things that we missed. Now happy?"

And he playfully stroked Juanita's chin. She was forced to smile.

But she was determined to find out. Yes she would today. Now or never.

———◆———

Adolfo slammed the flung his coat upon the wicker work table. Pablo sat on the bed grinning like a perfect idiot. Upon seeing Adolfo his grin widened making him look like a frog trying to please his missus.

"Well Adolfo, looks like your bitch has sniffed up something. Isn't it?"

"Aw….... Come on, she's devoted to me. She won't suspect a thing she's not of that type".

"But how long more can we carry on like this sweetheart".

"We may have to shift after a day as two. But let tomorrows be tomorrows. Let us think about tonight."

Adolfo removed his silk shirt and came down and lay beside Pablo. He was undoing his pants.

"You know one thing Pablo. The world can accept a gay footballer. The world can accept a gay engineer. The world can accept a gay lawyer. But he won't accept a gay doctor or a gay commissar. But why? Are we not human beings? What if God made us like that? It is his fault and we get punished Not that I like doing this to her. But got no choice. Need a cover to be safe. What a pity."

Adolfo sighed.

Juanita's blood froze.

Her hands were trembling uncontrollably. She urged, cajoled and implored to her hand to stay still, to stay still to hold the gun rock steady as she sent a pellet of searing death into the heart of that heartless demon, to suck away his life-blood, into the heart of that cheat who had insulted her love, ravaged her emotions, and raped her soul. It is the heart of the fiend who mocked her youth, who ravished her virginity, who bled her faith. Into the heart of the one who destroyed her life.

The very oak door that veiled her lover's unworthy acts loomed before her. The very key hole through which she had heard her death sentence, stared right into her eye.

She was going to go. She now had to go. She did not want to stay anymore. But she was not going to go alone. She had always craved for company.

She steadied her hand and knocked the door.

There was a rustle and a soft murmur amplified by the pervading silence. Clothes were rearranged. The big door yawned open with a somnolent creak. Juanita pointed the revolver point blank into the eyes of Adolfo. Her delicate finger curled around the trigger and wrestled with it, literally. Try as hard as she might she could not bear to mess up the beautiful face. She simply stared into it, bewitched.

There was a shuffle and a pounce. Juanita sidestepped. Pablo was flung face down on the carpet; his attempted lunge on the gun had miserably misfired. Slowly he tried to turn around. Juanita couldn't bear to see his face again. She shot him in the back of the head. Death was instantaneous. A slight shudder, then twitching of leg muscles as life force vaporized. And then stillness.

Muzzle turned back to Adolfo. Juanita's eyes turned back to his face. She still couldn't mess it up. She stood mesmerized. She did not see the hand whip out a Colt. She did not even see it being leveled. A bang was what she heard last. A slap in the fore head was what she felt last.

"Kill my lover….. you bitch". Adolfo spat in the bloodied face of Juanita.

Chapter 26

Extract from Juan's Diary.

"I was young. Reasonably good looking and had quite some money at my disposal. I had friends. Lots of them. Eusavio, Florio, Cletus, Remo and who not. I enjoyed many things with them. I loved those seemingly endless talk sessions. In front of my house or my friend's house. We start with girls, move on to politics and end up in sports. Time consumed, 3 full hours. Then Eusavio says he must be going. Okay I say. I escort him to the driveway. In the middle of the way, amidst pink blooms and stars and moon he is reminded of a new sportsman in the senior league. Again we start off on our long unending journey this time starting with sports and ending on girls with a slight touch of sports. Finally Eusavio says again, "I must be going". He goes up to his bike I accompany him to the road. And another talk session there. Total time few hours. Same with Florio, same with Remo and so on. Ma never really minds this nonsense as long as it keeps me off drugs and things of that sort.

But I managed to fool her. I enjoyed all the prohibitables (sic) with my friends…….. smoke, booze, grass. But no brothels. It was not that I did not have normal sex desires.

It was also not that I had bouts of moral phobias. Just the concept of paying women for sex was both discomforting and belittling for me.

It was as if the man had nothing to offer during sex and all his organs were worthless from the female point of view. More than that, his organs were an unwelcome intrusion into her privacy, which only could be entertained at a cost. The man must pay for the useful time of the woman he had wasted for his whims. Nothing was more disgraceful for man. I also disliked the creator for creating such a world where women call all the shots in sex. Where women's beautiful body is only appreciated by fellow men. But just look at the monopoly of women. The scales were really tipped in their favor and it was unjust in my opinion.

I thought that I was to stay an eternal virgin. But that was before Vera came into my life…….."

Chapter 27

Star News Nov-15 Wednesday- Obituary

Medellin:- Juanita Adolfo Jara, wife of police commissioner Mr. Adolfo Jara died after a brief illness at her residence at Salt Lake Reclamation yesterday. The body is lying in state at the Xavier's medical college after postmortem. The Ministry of defense, the Superintendant (operations) Northern Command and Home Ministry have all condoned the untimely death of Mrs. O. Jara. Family sources did not reveal much about the illness or the circumstances of death. Mr. O. Jara was too shocked by this immense personal loss to give any reaction. Friends and close associates describe him as being immensely in love with his beautiful wife and say that the Mr. Jara has since been moving about as if in a daze. The burial and service shall be tomorrow at 5.30 PM according to family sources.

Daily Herald – Special City Report

Medellin Nov-15 Wednesday
A male prostitute and a known frequenter of Black Pearl was found dead in a dustbin off Main road near Cathedral.

Forensic examinations have revealed that there were traces of semen in his anus. The apparent cause of death was a gun shot in the back of head. Police are investigating and are trying to ascertain the reason for murder and a manhunt is on for the killer. The deceased has been identified by preliminary investigations as Pablo. Further details are awaited.

He knew it. The two newspaper reports. Words were still fresh in his head like yesterdays dew-drops. The whole scene unfolded before his eyes like a pantomime. And he was the lone spectator. The lone spectator who watched with vengeful intensity as his sister was cheated, used and then dumped like a toilet paper by an unscrupulous monster. His brain was ablaze.

He believed that his hair was on fire.

Chapter 28

"Myself Me .....What a fool am I. There is no God. Even if there is God he is an invalid. He is a cretin, a mentally and physically handicapped wreck. He got no eyes, no ears. He sees nothing, he hears not the plaintiff calls of the faithful. What is the use of such a God? A God who relaxes in heaven while his children bleed? Like a promiscuous rich man who is perpetually in between the legs of his concubines while his unwanted, unwarranted for bastards grovel and cry in the streets. Yes. Bastards. That is what we are. Children whom god created without any purpose. By-products of a wanton whim. Remnants of divine recklessness."

"For the last time I snuff out the name of God from my system. In the name God I swear that I don't believe in God any more. No, I am mistaken. In the name of Satan.... Oh God help me. No-No Oh Satan give me strength. You are my master from this moment onwards. Accept me, My Lord, My Master, Master of the Universe."

Juan broke down sobbing uncontrollably. The walls responded with grim silence. The window opened into a vast darkness. Night had set in.

Clouds devoured the moon and the stars.

Chapter 29

Only a trained contract killer can scale a two storey high building in a pitch dark night with the help of a rope. Only a trained contract killer can noiselessly open glass windows bolted from inside without attracting attention of guards below. Only a killer can step into a post autopsy morgue and delve through dead bodies mangled beyond repair.

Yes, this was Juanita's body all right. It was in one piece. No autopsy had been performed. Juan tenderly lifted the shroud. A neatly punched hole blushed crimson. He clenched his fists.

Fully clad in insulating rubber, and camouflaged against the ink of night, he proceeded to cut the energized wires. Before snapping each link he would short circuit the wire with a long cable that looped safely behind him. He knew that lest he break the circuit in even a single wire of the fence, the alarms would be set off.

Today was Juanita's burial.

Adolfo had to be laid to rest with her.

Not one more sun should shine into his life. So he had to be careful. Only one more wire had to be cut. Carefully he wrapped the naked ending of the cable he was carrying about one metes to the left of his entry point. He looped the insulated part behind him in the grass. The other end he connected one meter to the right of his target area. Now he could snap the wire without breaking the circuit. The clipper clicked.

Revenge entered.

The window to the hall was unguarded. There were no dogs. The police obviously put too much faith in their electric fence. Two guards tried to disseminate the boredom with puffs of cigar smoke and baseless banter. Their chatter made the job easier. Panes were cut. The door softly opened. Juan entered. The panes were replaced with fast drying resin. Before him were thick blinds. Soft light filtered through the myriad pores in the blind. It afforded a hazy view of the hall.

"Just about Right Place," thought Juan. He softly screwed on the silencer and double checked the bullets. Now he had to wait.

The force with which the door was precipitated against the wood work necessitated a loud bang.

Juan stiffened.

"Mister Adolfo, you never loved your wife. Then why be sullen? Throw away this grief and join me in an Aperitif".

Corlios uncorked a new bottle of sparkling red wire.

"To shucks birth that bitch Juanita. To hell with her, really to hell with her. Who grieves for her? Good riddance. And the bastard robbed me of Pablo. Life will never be the same again. She has wrecked me. That scheming merciless bitch". Adolfo was beside himself with consummate pseudo pious rage. His glass trembled and some scarlet liquid fell down.

Behind the curtain Juan bristled. Never before had anybody used such utterly base references for his beautiful darling Juanita with impunity.

"Bastard, I'll spill your blood on the very wine you drop. And I'll mix the two and drink an aperitif to the soul of my sister. I promise you. Just wait."

"Corlios, the night is warm Isn't it?

"It's just that the room is suffocating stuffy. Why don't you open the windows".

"Good Idea. Should lighten the load of this room and of my mind perhaps".

He strode to the window and removed the blind with a flourish. And his jaw dropped and eyes popped out.

And there were two mild pops.

It was a funny sight. Adolfo lay, still staring at ceiling with a confused expression on his face. His eyes were still staring out. Only a third eye now gaped in between the two. A crimson one. How funny? Three Eyes….. Hah! Corlios lay prostrate before the liquor cabinet as though paying obeisance to some spirit. The back of his nape was punched neatly. His blood was not distinguishable from the red wine. His nose had got stuck in a bottle as he was slammed forward by the impact of the slug. A funny sight indeed and Juan laughed. He laughed loud and clear. He laughed as he had never done before. A funny sight indeed.

He had never laughed before at the sight of slain men.
He slayed men, but never for once did he find death
amusing. The sight of his Victims always had filled him

*with remorse. But not now. Now he laughed. Real Joke,
The two men and their funny last stands and stances.*

*He knew that at last his new master had accepted
him.................. He was one with him now.*

Long billowy fingers of nicotine rich smoke crawled up
the heavy air for a rendezvous with the nonchalant ceiling.

*"Yes, I remember. Clearly Juanita had said don't kill
Adolfo on orders. Exactly that is what her words were.
So I didn't break my word. I didn't kill Adolfo on orders.
My conscience is clear".*

*"But wait. What if my conscience is not clean. It
need not be clear any more. Even if I had broken my
promise, so what? Praise be my new Lord. It's all so
convenient now".*

Juan blow out the smoke with a new found vengeance.

*"Father was right. Even Juanita is not among the one
in a million" Damn it. Father is always correct. I only
wish I could disprove him for once. Just for once. But
then what if not? To hell with father and his bullshit.
After all it is so convenient now".*

Chapter 30

Juan's Lamborghini slid effortlessly along the smooth tarmac. Adroit hands, adept at anything mechanical, caressed and cajoled the willing steering effortlessly as Juan's brain shifted to fourth gear and thoughts raced by his mind as if vying with the fleeting impressions of giant glass and concrete edifices blurring past his eye.

"A call from head quarters. Got to be something important. No parceled instructions. A top priority crack shot is on. Would be nice to see old Muso again."

Juan chuckled to himself as he remembered how Muso had quivered and sniveled like a cornered mouse during their last meeting.

"I hope he has dumped all that. Any way he has to. I'm the best that the Family has got. He can't afford to fiddle with me. In a way he is more dispensable than I am."

The smile that graced Juan's grim countenance was one of tremendous satisfaction and happiness. Ever since inception he had been told and told repeatedly that, by-products of the cheapest possible and the only affordable entertainment in shanty town like him, never mattered. Now that he did, was a step forward, indeed.

Juan grinded the car into a halt and indeed the light from huge signboard of coffee trading house ricocheted unpleasantly off his eye-balls. This was a flaw in its design, that he had always noticed and never cared for really. His mind could simultaneously process instructions from two sources. In the church school, his mind would be somewhere else, but still he would take down the notes word for word without the hint of a mistake without even knowing it. He noticed it now also and as usual he didn't care. He never noticed any special qualities about himself. Shanty town by-products were never taught to delve into themselves to unearth hidden talents and aptitudes. They were never really meant for that.

"Coffee-Board!, Indeed Cocaine in the skin of coffee", Juan mused aloud as he banged the Lamborghini shut and strode up the marble stairs that led to the tinted glass entrance.

Inside were oak, mahogany, teak, ebony and precious metal. All up in arms, celebrating the shameless profligacy of ill-gotten wealth. A concentrated resplendence of Persian carpets led up to the glass elevator. Juan glided in and pressed third floor.

The silver was there. The rich paneling was there. Expensive Van Gogh's and Picasso's were also there. The gold in laid table was there alright. They were always there. The cigar was there, but it was a local brand. It existed clasped firmly in the stubby, lard filled fingers of Muso.

But its roots did not lie in Havana. One small indication that the stars were not so benevolent for the Cartel anymore. Pressure from United States of America

was beginning to tell. The Havana Cigars had been steam-rolled by the American juggernaut.

Muso motioned Juan to sit and adjusted his horn-rimmed glass. He took one deep draught from the cigar to clear his mind. He had intended this meeting to be as crystal clear as possible.

Muso cleared his throat and steadied himself.

"Well, my dear boy. You are aware of what is happening in our principal market, I presume."

Muso's directness came as no shock to Juan. He knew that pressure from the States was mounting. All knew of it.

"Yes I do"

"You must also be aware that our unpatriotic government is toeing the aggressor's line. Let me make it clear. Francis. Francis-La-Fontaine, the man who handles American trade has been arrested."

This was nothing perturbing.

"So what? Our men do get arrested once in a while. The government also wants its share of profits. Just give it to them and end the matter as usual."

"Well", Muso cleared his throat. Once again and coughed up a substantial phlegm. Chain smoking was taking its toll.

"As I was saying. The situation is different now. A case has been framed and evidence has been dossiered."

Now Juan could sense trouble.

"What will be the implications if he is convicted".

"It means that our operations in Americas are rudderless. At least for the time being. Plain and simple. And you know how much time being will cost. We simply can't afford it. America is our principal market. Loss of United States means no bread and butter for the cartel and it means no bread and butter for me and you. You understand?"

"Yes true, I can see. But weren't all the officials and judges our brothers?"

"That is the tragedy. It is Satan's sway now boy, brother backstabs brother, Father slays son, and mothers poison infants.

All for money. They have all been bought. The government, the officials, the judges. The traitors, those mother fucking bastards. They have all been bought by the United States. We cannot match their dollar power".

"Yes true. I know that the Satan part is true. But what do we do from here".

"Send a message. A clear message, an unequivocal message, that we tolerate no nonsense. For years those fucking leeches have lived off us. And now if they double cross us, we fuck them alive. That is what?"

"Great spirit. But where do I fit in into all this?

"Exactly, that is what we are here about. Let me be short and clear. Judge Gonzales is going to hear Francis' case in the sessions on December the twenty sixth, the day after the Christmas holidays. Today is December the thirteenth. You blow him within twelve days. And the offer is, after this you get a choice of termination of your contract and a life-time pension and also the choice to continue."

For a moment Juan went blank. The name Gonzales had left his mind numbed empty.

And then the floodgates opened. Hazy memories. Vera, Her eventual husband Judge Gonzales, his infatuation for her, her practice sessions with him, the way he was used and dumped.

Victory of money over man.

It all swam and whirled around him in a dizzying incessant cesspool into which he was drowning deeper and deeper. And then all of a sudden uncontrollable raze boiled and overpowered him. He shook and shivered. His nails clawed into the leather upholstery and teeth locked in a grinding embrace. Hot sweat poured down his nose. The cloud burst was evident on his face. Muso noticed it.

"That's the spirit boy. That's it and I assure that we all share this deep hatred for our fucking traitors and those American pigs".

"It's not that", Juan's protest sounded feeble against his bellicose countenance.

"Then what?" Muso was frankly taken aback by Juan's clarification.

"Never mind." Juan's tone was more relaxed. His years in the "definitive Adieus" job had trained him to suppress emotions fast and wholesome.

"As you say", Muso was non committal. Cartel's rules prohibited intrusion into the privacy of any member however infinitesimal it was.

"Collect the dossier from Clara and make sure you learn well. This is top important, study and learn well. This is top important and no scope for levity whatsoever. And no space for failure either. I hope you understand."

"Perfectly, Sir"

"Good", Muso smiled for the first time that evening.

"So definitive adios for Gonzalez by December the twenty fifth. Right?"

"Right Boss" Juan tried to infuse as much confidence as he could into his voice. It was Friday the thirteenth. Juan was never much superstitious, but somehow he did not feel all right this day.

"Friday, Thirteenth, Vera, Gonzalez could be the end". These thoughts kept ringing again and again in his mind like a stuck record.

"Right Boss" the words trailed past him. He wasn't very convinced. But Senor Muso was. Through confused eyes Juan saw him smile yet once again. He was glad that he did.

Juan closed the dossier with a resolute bang and took another deep draught of whisky with warm water.

Chapter 31

"Bullet proof Car - American supplied of course. Twenty four hour escort. Inaccessible house..................... I know the remedy. The anti-dote. I shall send shards those very glasses meant to protect him, to shred him into pieces. And I have it with me".

"A self propelled limpet impact mine clinging to the very glass that was meant to save his life. The Steel of the Car body would be irresistible to the Limpet!!!! That's the way to do it .... But how? How do I get the Mine there ....That is the question?"

He took another draught and poured in more whiskey.

Then he proceeded to milk his grey cells, trying to wring out some likeness of a concrete plan from them. He had to. And respond they did. The intense onslaught of the ambrosia of stimulant called whisky and intense desire called Juan was too much for the recalcitrant grey cells. They succumbed to his desires.

"The launch pad will be a 500 ccs Kawasaki. The launcher shall be concealed behind its massive headlights. Sights shall be a video camera integrated into the launcher. Its display unit will be hid in the speedometer console. Trigger shall be incorporated into the horn. And a Kawasaki

500 CC should be enough for a fast get-away. But where should the ambush take place …let me think…think …head please think fast …"

"Bravo" Juan congratulated himself aloud. But he knew the job was only half done. But "Where" was a big problem. "No problem" thought Juan. A map of the Judge's daily route was provided with the dossier. Now what he needed was a straight stretch of road with a convenient diversion a few seconds after the place, from where, he would launch the limpet mine. After that it would be one mad dash through the diversion. The road had to be straight. Airplane Runway Straight. ***Rocket propelled limpets cannot negotiate curves. And he would not be getting enough time to remote control it to the target.***

"Yes that is it. Vasco-da-gama Avenue would be just fine. Two diversions at Church Gate intersection. Just right"

He took a piece of paper and jolted down the details of his strike motorbike. The Cartel people should have it ready within a week he believed. After writing he rubbed his hands in glee.

Sure, this was going to be the second killing that he was going to really enjoy in two months.

The Cartel was more efficient than what he had expected. The death machine was ready and delivered within four days complete with complement of ten rocket propelled limpet mines.

Juan was honestly taken aback by the quality of stuff provided and the awesome firepower that had been granted to him. The mines were really top grade. The mines were Swedish make, Carl Gustafson with stabilized fins, twin engines and incorporating state of the art Thorpe E.M.I electronic adjustable firing device. The rocket pod was mounted in the sleek head lamp and the aiming device assimilated in the speedometer as specified. There was a spare assembly for emergency situated under the tank. The video scanner, range finders and triggers were all Thorpe E.M.I, the best in the world, standard equipment for NATO's Rapid Deployment Force. Juan marveled, awe-struck at the resourcefulness and the reach of the cartel. They had procured the best in the world at such a short notice. Surely it would take more than just plain determination to destroy such an organization. He really felt proud to be a part of it. Or at least for the moment.

"Now for the trials, We have enough ammo spare" thought Juan with a satisfied smile.

Chapter 32

The field trials went perfect.

It was in the jungles to the south of Medellin, absolute hundred percent Cartel Country. A man drove a battered limousine with bullet proof glass in the rear vane. Juan followed in his attack vehicle at about hundred meters. The moment they reached the clearing, the limousine was revved up and the driver bailed out.

Meanwhile Juan had adjusted the sights of the video aimer sights straight at the rear pane. As soon as the window appeared neat and clear in between the cross mark of the screen he pressed the trigger. With a deafening whoosh the mine launched itself at the Limo. A few seconds later impact and then one second and an ear splatting explosion wrecked havoc on the morning tranquility. Shrieking birds arose, dust settled.

Juan and Muso and others strode unmindful of the racket, towards the mutilated car that lay precipitated against a tree, engine still running.

Carefully Juan opened the door and shut the engine. Then they all looked inside.

Juan's calculations were perfect. Thousands of small pieces of hardened glass, each transformed into a lethal projectile by the explosion had played havoc with the interior. The upholstery, the dash board, the steering were all a tattered mangled heap. The glass projectiles had broken all hell loose with such vengeance that they punched neat holes in the driver's seat. All occupants, if any would have been torn to shreds, decimated beyond recognition by that deadly hail of super energized hardened glass splinters. There would be no survivors, it was clear.

"Fabulous, Great, Fantastic, Marvelous" Muso was still searching for words to express his immense appreciation, as an assistant doused the mangled wreck that was once a car with gasoline and set it alight.

"I knew he could do it. He would bring out the perfect plan. He is the best we have got".

Muso was gasping and gulping with excitement, his fallow face red with the effort. He swept Juan with an affectionate glance and smiled broadly.

"I need not say anything more. You are perfect by yourself. So the time is up to you. But before December the twenty sixth. Okay? And one more thing, Merry Christmas. I have some work in Lima. May be we won't meet again before Christmas." The helicopter was already revving up eager to master the skies it owned.

"Thank you Sir, and same to you."

With a mighty defiant roar the giant bird took to the skies while its lesser contemporaries scattered in fright. Juan kicked his Kawasaki to a throbbing shuddering start.

Chapter 33

"Sun was madly ravaging the barren lifeless tract. No vegetation met the eye, spare the thorny parched shrubs. The thorns were larger than the leaves,-.... much larger and red.

Juan Stared unblinking, at the mottled green, laced with painful yellow of the death throes and mummified dead brown of the already wasted pathetic leaves, was completely dwarfed by the vengeful, blood- thirsty bloody red of the thorns.

The cruel sun cloaked the blood soaked thorns in sinful magnificence. And the whittled leaves, life-sap slowly draining, quivered and whimpered, praying for mercy, from the obnoxious hellish heat bent upon destroying them. A huge dry depression, that was once a life giving beautiful thriving lake, stood to his left, its bosom barren and bared, its heart lifeless.

Vera clasped Juan's legs in a vice like grip. Her hair was pathetically tousled and woeful tears glistened down her cheeks.

"Mercy, Mercy. Please don't kill him".

She prayed.

Juan looked at Vera, and then at the huge knife in his hand, already crimson in eager anticipation of the libation of life blood it was about to receive.

Then his eyes fell of Gonzalez lying at his feet tied up and helpless. His resolve grew only firmer. He had to take revenge, show Vera what he was made of, and drink the blood of the man, who by the power of wealth had taken away the object of his carnal desires.

Now the power was in his hands. He was duty bound to power to take away his victim's life. Power demanded its misuse. As it had been previously misused upon him. His pride demanded Gonzalez's blood. His libido demanded Gonzalez's blood.

"Let go" Juan bellowed but Vera clung on with greater resolve. Summoning the beast within him, he heaved forward dragging Vera with him. The blood red thorns knifed through her petite frame and hot blood spurted out. Some of it fell on Juan's face. It was refreshing. Juan licked the blood on his lips. It was exhilarating, a heady Aphrodisiac for the things to come. He could have slayed Vera. But he had other plans for her.

He raised his huge knife, the fiendish blade glinting with demoniac satisfaction, and aimed it straight at Gonzalez's heart.

There was a blinding flash and suddenly a towering luminosity appeared before Juan. Desperately he tried to shield his eyes from all pervading luminescence of the being with the evil blade of his knife. But try as hard as he might, the light still filtered through.

"Stop, Juan stop". A voice from within the luminosity commanded. It was less of a command and more of a gentle admonishment.

"No, I won't, I swear I won't, Get Away, let me do my job. Don't intervene, Please don't". Juan was screaming hysterically.

"Take a look at your feet". The voice was as gentle as ever.

Juan looked and was numbed aghast. To his one feet clung a bloodied Juanita. To his other feet clung his desperate mother. Crying, pleading, praying, faces devastated beyond recognition, bodies bruised beyond repair.

"Spare our husbands" they cried in unison and disappeared.

The huge knife slid slowly from Juan's hand and his clenched fists uncoiled. Suddenly the brightness was no more blinding.

"Take a look back" the voice again said.

Juan heeded. And lo behold, there were unexpected surprises galore.

The leaves were growing and the thorns were shrinking soon the leaves grew to their fullest emerald iridescence. One by one the thorns wilted and fell. The desert now was a vast expanse of luminescent vibrancy. Birds were singing and in the distance he could see children playing. The sun was bright but now the brightness did not hurt. The warmth was soft, nurturing and life giving. Paradise was reborn.

Juan felt thirsty, very thirsty. Wearily he looked at the dry lake to his left. It had disappeared. It had reappeared to his right, huge and bountiful, rimming with, sweet rippling crystal clear water.

Juan stooped down and drank and drank. Now his heart was full. Presently he stood up. A small island had appeared at the centre of the lake. The gentle melodious voice of a child praying wafted into his ears. The sound seemed to come from the island. Juan decided to investigate. A number of boats were moored all around the lake. They all had mysterious symbols on them. One of the symbols was familiar. It was the cross.

Juan decided to take the boat with the cross on it. He pushed it into the gentle waters and began rowing towards the island.

The island was even more beautiful than the paradise he had left behind. Or was this paradise? Beautiful flowers, beautiful trees, beautiful birds, beauty everywhere. The colors were bright but not vulgar. Their iridescence was soothing. The wind was brisk but not violent. Their credo was to soothe the sweat of the tired traveler. The sounds were loud and clear but not painful. They were melodious beyond comparison.

Noiselessly Juan beached the boat and made way towards the source of the sound. In a clearing in the island, surrounded by trees and flowers of indescribable beauty and dignity, stood a virgin white statue of Madonna suckling little Jesus.

Mother Mary's face had such a serene and contented look that it brought tears into Juan's eyes. At her feet knelt a little boy with folded hands sweetly reciting his prayers. Juan was determined to find out who he was. Slowly he tiptoed up to him .... And gasped as he recognized him....

Chapter 34

Cold sweat broke on his forehead as Juan was rudely jolted out of his slumber. The dream was etched deep in his mind and soul in graphic detail. He lit a cigarette. The dense smoke enshrouded him to blanket his self from outside interference as mind subjected itself to deep thought.

Soliloquy -:

"I cannot do it. I simply cannot, for God's sake. I cannot destroy my love's happiness although she does not deserve it. Let a thousand beings err, but not shall I. Now I can see clearly.

I was simply not made to err. God had much noble intentions when he created me. And there is only one way out. I must go.

And it's no matter too. No matter, that I got no woman, pop, brother sister, no love, no peace, nobody to love me and make me feel wanted. So I go, no matter. Mother earth will be only too glad to have unwanted people like me off her back, she is already too burdened. One less, one less stomach, one less polluter, one less exploiter of her. One less to take away, what legitimately belongs to her other creatures. Already there are many of by-products. Us.

But it cannot end like this. The D-Costa blood line cannot end here. Me. After me who...? I have to plant a seed before I go. But then who in this world would accept a dying man's sperm? Which women would bear a condemned mans child, rearing it up? And after my end. Then our lineage ends. Brother, sister all gone without continuation. It is now my holy duty to see that it continues.

This is my solemn duty towards my good father, my blessed forefathers. The lineage must go on. And it must be a blessed one too. There aren't many who think unselfish like me, who love unselfish like me. And god would not mind another of it. Nor would mother earth I'm sure. In fact she desperately needs more like us.

So I have to plant a seed before I go. And plant it where it will be nurtured, cherished and grown with loving care most dutifully. I should plant it where the sapling will not feel an unwanted by-product like me but a cherished and wanted living creature with life and soul. But where?

Who in this world would accept a dying man's sperm?

Kind divine Father, you who told me so much about myself, now please tell me were. Please answer. Your silence will break a dying man's heart and his sadness will curse you so that you too will be unwanted on earth.

...Yes, I see it now. A repentant hooker. A lady forced into it. A lady who loves god and hates what she does. And is willing to do anything to be free. Yes a repentant unwilling flesh purveyor. Thank you my Lord. I know you would never fail me when it mattered. You have never did."

In my heart of hearts I know it. I know I would disprove my father. Hear me father, I am the one in a million that you said, I am the one in a million chosen by my lord to do him the ultimate service. I'm the chosen one."

"Oh My Lord, Oh my Merciful Father in the Heaven, I Juan Carlos D Costa absolve myself from and relinquish all my mortal Contracts and renew my Contract with You...... and this time I promise you there shall be no violations ....I swear in the name of my forefathers and in the name of the flesh, blood and tears of your only begotten son...I swear"

He was hollering the empty space above his head and the stoic cold ceiling beyond.

Chapter 35

She was simply thrashing away at his genitals. He lay there staring emptily into the space as she sat over him straddling him between her legs. His hips swayed to and fro as though detached from the rest of his body...... and soul.

"Now don't stare at the ceiling", her tingling voice was hoarse and husky. But the pretence in it clearly filtered through the mask of simulated excitement. At least Juan could not be fooled so easily.

"Look at my crotch. Look at this fuzz. look here". She pointed at the wet concavity that was intermittently sucking in and regurgitating his hardness like a child playing with a lolli-pop.

"Looking makes it more fun", she continued in her hoarse frequency. "And just let me know when you are to come. I'll show you a new trick.'

"I think it is time". Juan replied without even thinking. Almost immediately the whore stopped swaying and extracted Juan from herself. Gently she placed pressed the glans penis. White fluid spurted out and spread all over her pubis.

"Oh dear" she cried in mock disappointment," the precious liquid did not reach where it was required. Now what shall I do?" She laughed shrilly and spread her legs wide apart so that everything could be seen and sighed loudly. Then giggling and moaning softly, with a soft sinuous motion she used Juan's manhood to spoon up a little sticky fluid and inserted it into her vagina and rolled her hips, as if spreading it evenly inside slowly. Groaning and moaning in mock pleasure, she transferred all of it into within herself and then lay beside him.

"That was nice?" she giggled.

"Yes Pretty good". Juan's tone was surprisingly genuinely detached. Indeed his thoughts were elsewhere.

"Not the one I am looking for. Three full days of scouring and still not the one I am looking for.'

He sighed softly.

Chapter 36

"I'll be in a minute sir. Please make yourself comfortable."

The joyousness was feigned as usual but it was also blended with a tinge of remorse. Saying this she went inside.

The hint of remorse sent a small tingle of excitement through Juan's spine. Was this the one? He had to know. He tiptoed after her.

There she was, kneeling before an altar. And in the soft light her clear face looked yes, virginal. *The whore actually looked virginal when she prayed*. Juan studied her carefully. Her features were handsome, though not exactly beautiful. There was grace, dignity, the way her eyelids fluttered, a quiet hint of character the way her lips trembled, a purity in her being. She stood up and looked back. And saw Juan staring intently at her. For a moment she blushed and then steadied herself.

A prostitute's face flushing was heartwarming to Juan.

"Now business", she smiled with as much gay abandon as she could muster."

"Yes true yes true but what and why? I mean what you were doing now?".

"Now that shouldn't interest you, I'm sure. Besides you are here for business. Aren't you?"

Her tone was defensive.

"Yes true, But I insist to know. I assure you this is no plain curiosity. It is important. Please."

Carista took one long look at Juan's earnest face and then gazed at her toes.

"If you insist well okay, yes. The fact is I don't like this whole business of selling love. Love is to be felt, not sold. Praying before I do it makes me feel better. I give a better performance. Satisfying my customers is also my duty isn't it?'

"Well yes. But this means you in fact don't like what you do. Right?"

Juan was fighting to submerge the excitement crawling up his tone.

"I doubt if anybody does".

"Now you are not to judge that. But leave it. That me why do it if you don't love it".

"Bread my friend. Bread. No choice, we the poor have only two places for bread in here. Either kill or sell. I though selling was better than killing".

"I know that the kill or sell is true. But what if you get a choice? I mean a choice between kill-sell and not kill-sell. I mean with good holy pure bread for the rest of your life".

"There is no choice Mister. Here we have no choice".

There was dejection, disappointment and rage in her words. And they were not feigned.

Juan felt sad, for he knew she was justified in her angst. The same way that he was justified in his angst. It was the same hopelessness that made him rebel against his Lord. And she was justified in being angry, as justified as he was.

"I'll give you a choice, in fact an offer. I am talking real, believe me you got a choice. God is great. He gave you salvation and me a chance to repent by using my sinful wealth to prevent a pure being from being defiled further. I tell you Carista… God is great. He is really great. Praise be the almighty".

In one moment of pure thrill, he swept her in his arms and warmly kissed her cheeks.

Her cheeks, not her lips, not her bosom, not her in-betweens.

What an uncustomary thing to do.

Chapter 37

They were both sitting in the lounge of the department of gynecology and obstetrics. Mr. and Mrs. McNamara the register book said so.

Carista was sobbing softly. Her languid wistful eyes searched Juan's moist brethren for answers.

"What if the test comes true?"

Juan held her hands tenderly. Never before had he felt so affectionate. At least not recently. It seemed all his pent up affection had found a catharsis.

"It means God given us a both a chance to make amends. You make amends. Devote yourself to the child. Make sure he comes up a true son of god. Make him love mankind by loving him. Make him fell cherished, not a by-product."

"Face it, Carista........ We all have to play our part in his great ways for sanctity of his realm. And he, who showed us the path, shall give us the courage to tread it. Have confidence in him."

"Congratulations Mr. and Mrs. What you said, yes Mr. McNamara. The test is positive. I know you will be delighted for nobody wanted to be parents like you two. Imagine four visits here, on four consecutive days".

Carista shuddered. Juan exulted.

Chapter 38

The cavalcade grandly coasted along the highway. Massive steel and glass towers, their facades glittering in expensive resplendence stood mute witness.

Grand Judge Gonzalez was on his way to the church. The Christmas mass was on.

There ware festivities galore on the fourth link road. Christmas spirit was at his bountiful best. The world was a celebration of colors. Festoons, cutouts strings of balloons, all contributed their mirthful might to the riot of effulgence. People shopping, shoving, treading on others toes, children hollering, mothers straining, fathers tugging, youngsters as carefree as ever-. Everything was lively, pulsating, throbbing with the joy of life.

And nobody noticed a superbly styled battle cat of a motor bike parked innocuously beside a café and nobody really bothered to mind the young man in dark overalls and a visor on it. Christmas is really intoxicating. A day when nobody suspects nobody, when nobody minds nobody,….. yet everybody cares.

Juan checked his video sights. The trained them at the bonnet of a car about hundred yards away.

Intently he peered at the dial.

And from nowhere an angelic little boy appeared in front of the bonnet. Yes, the cross of the sight had an angelic, captivating, radiant young boy behind it – The Rays of the sun appeared to form a Halo behind his enchantingly fetching and winsome countenance. -----Presently the child aimed a cherubic smile straight at the camera and the smile flooded the sights.

The sepulchral ululation of the Sirens of the lead car clashed acrimoniously with the joyous sounds of celebration.

The battle cat shuddered into life with a recalcitrant growl. An unholy altercation of rubber with asphalt and the journey had begun.

The white bike raced after the black car. A phosphorescent flash and a luminous satellite detached from the mother vehicle and tore apart the languid air.

A tongue of flame snaked towards a steel water tank overhead. A few seconds later there was a thunderous explosion. But there was no fire of hate, no inferno of death.

Only a cool cascade of refreshing liquid and steam where libations of compassion doused the flames of vengeance.

Guards in the Escort Cars turned. Machine guns exploded into a staccato. The maddening crescendo tore asunder the presiding peace and drove it helter skelter.

And an idealist had paid the price for his idealism. The price for striving for ideals in a cynical time. Price for trying to be perfect in a patently nihilistic world of sinners who do not tolerate outsiders.

Chapter 39

A small lamp dispels the pervading darkness in a room on Pensioner's Hill.

It always keeps burning. There is a portrait before it on an Altar.

The Oil of Holy Faith and milk of Human Kindness nurses and nurtures this little lamp. A tiny little lamp that fights back the monstrous gargantuan juggernaut of black around it.

"A tiny little David, with the temerity to challenge the Goliaths of this creation".

There are no Electric bulbs in this room. Only the lamp, the portrait and the darkness....

And the battle rages on ....and on ....and on.

The lamp never dies.

Carista would never ever let it die.

I hope she never ever does.

-The End-